Story Of Two

BY
Yvette Way

Symphony 18 Publishing

Cover design by NubianFX

Copyright © 2022 By Joanna Holloway

All rights reserved. No part of this book may be used or reproduced by any means including photocopying, recording, taping, or by any information storage retrieval system without the written permission of the publisher except in case of brief quotations embodied in critical articles or reviews.

This is a work of fiction. All characters, names, incidents, organizations, and dialogue in this novel are either products of the author's imagination or are used fictitiously.

ISBN: 979-8-988-36620-1(pbk)

Acknowledgements:

My first acknowledgement is to a place and its occupants. This place was a constant in a world of change. It was also a place that contributed to my growth as a person. I will not mourn this place; I will celebrate it and its former occupants. The place, 18 Symphony Road.

I also, like I said, would like to acknowledge the former occupants, including my mother, aunts, cousins, uncles, and nana. And so many others who made my time there a learning, loving, and growing experience.

I also want to acknowledge my other family and friends who have joined me on this journey called life. I love you and thank you.

Chapter 1

Jocelyn and Terrell have never been alone in their relationship. Throughout an off and on relationship everyone has always had an opinion on how they should live their life, what is acceptable and what is not acceptable. Jocelyn's mom thought Terrell wasn't good enough for her. Terrell's mother thought that Jocelyn was selfish and wouldn't make a good wife or mother. "She's a career woman. You don't want that. If she doesn't have time for you now, do you think she's going to have time when she becomes a lawyer?" Terrell's mother used to tell him. Unfortunately for Jocelyn and Terrell, they didn't learn to ignore the opinions of outsiders.

Something out of nothing was everyone's motto when it came to her and Terrell's relationship, Jocelyn thought. It was so funny how people saw the littlest things in their relationship but couldn't see their own relationships falling apart around them. Jocelyn could never understand that.

She thought back and heard all the voices that told her they wouldn't last. That number was so high she lost count. For the most part they all had different reasons, but the most frequent reason was "he is not good enough for you". Some believed they wouldn't last because they were from different worlds. Others believed they wouldn't last because she was too ambitious, and he was happy to settle in his job. Some even suggested they were too much alike to be together for a long time.

What people never understood or did not talk about was the fact that they loved each other. It was the thing that kept them coming back to each other, despite everything that happened throughout their relationship. They threw caution to the wind when friends and family told them they were no good for each other.

It wasn't just outside influences that were the problem, they inflicted enough pain on each other. Insecurities and misunderstandings were among the reasons they couldn't keep it consistent. They didn't fight a lot, but they were both quick to break it off when they felt something was not right. They didn't communicate well. They finally agreed with the notion that it wasn't going to work out and they went their separate ways ten years ago.

To understand their relationship, there is no better place to start than at the beginning. Jocelyn met Terrell right after high school. Her best friend Monique saw him and thought that Jocelyn would like him. He was a friend of Monique's boyfriend. At Monique's constant urging Jocelyn finally agreed to meet him and Monique planned the meeting. All Jocelyn and Terrell had to do was show up.

Monique thought it would also be a good idea for them to talk before they met. She gave Terrell Jocelyn's phone number without telling Jocelyn. Jocelyn was mad at first but as they talked, she realized Terrell was cool and her anger subsided.

They talked nightly on the phone before they met. Jocelyn thought that even if it didn't work out Terrell was definitely someone she could see herself being friends with. Terrell made Jocelyn laugh a lot. She liked that but wondered if some of the things she laughed at were meant to make her laugh. If they weren't, he never corrected her.

Jocelyn went through five outfits the day they met. She was going for a casual look that was attractive and she decided on a red shirt with black jeans. She went through so many outfits and hairstyles she forgot about the time and ended up running late.

She arrived at Monique's house an hour late and Monique grilled her for it.

"Where were you? Why didn't you call if you knew you were going to be late? I thought you weren't coming. I would have killed you." Monique continued, "You're lucky he is nice and is still here. I personally would have left."

Jocelyn told her the bus was caught in traffic and it was beyond her control. Monique looked at Jocelyn. She wasn't buying it. She took Jocelyn's coat and saw what she had on, rolled her eyes and said, "What are you wearing?" At least Monique whispered this time. "You are so homely. You couldn't dress up?"

Jocelyn answered, "Why should I have dressed up? Are we going to dinner or something? I am only supposed to meet this guy. No one mentioned anything beyond that."

Monique shook her head and pushed Jocelyn up the stairs.

Jocelyn decided to mess with Monique. When she got to the top of the stairs, she saw Terrell sitting in the chair facing the other way but said, "There's no one here Monique. Where'd he go?"

Monique dashed up the stairs past Jocelyn and looked at the chair she left Terrell in. After seeing he was still there, she looked at Jocelyn with what started off as an angry look, but she couldn't help laughing.

They were still laughing when Monique introduced them. When Terrell stood up Jocelyn stopped laughing. She couldn't believe her eyes or his for that matter. He had the deepest, darkest brown eyes she had ever seen. His skin was also dark brown, the color of dark chocolate. Then he spoke and Jocelyn almost melted. His voice was deep, commanding and came out of a nice set of lips. She was definitely impressed by Terrell.

Monique sensed this and was grinning from ear to ear.

"Well, this is where I play hostess. Anyone want anything to drink or eat before I go?" Monique asked, still grinning.

Terrell asked for juice and Jocelyn said she was all set but when Monique returned, she returned with a glass of juice for Jocelyn also.

Jocelyn and Terrell talked for what seemed like hours. They didn't even notice that Monique's boyfriend Michael had come in and was standing over them. Michael, at the insistence of Monique, came into the living room to say hello. He had an unimpressed look on his face. As quickly as he appeared, he disappeared. Monique apologized for his behavior and followed him out of the room.

Jocelyn and Terrell just looked at each other and laughed at the whole situation and wondered why Michael was reacting the way he was. They shrugged his actions off with their laughter. They definitely had chemistry and they were hitting it off. Jocelyn was very pleasantly surprised.

Terrell took Jocelyn's glass of juice out of her hands and told her he had something important to ask her. She looked at him with concern because his facial expression was serious; she thought the worst.

"I've wanted to know something from the moment I met you," Terrell started. "Can I kiss you?"

Surprised and relieved Jocelyn answered, "Yep."

She was feeling extremely anxious.

"Are you sure you're ok with this?" Terrell asked after seeing the anxiety on her face.

"Yes, I'm ok with it. I don't know why I am so nervous, it's not like it's my first kiss." Jocelyn giggled and gave Terrell the perfect opening.

He kissed her in mid-laughter, and she couldn't catch her breath.

Yeah, she had kissed guys before, but it never felt like this. Thank God they were sitting down, she thought. Terrell looked at her for a moment, deep into her eyes. It was almost like he was trying to see through her. Then he kissed her again and again. This continued until Monique came into the room.

Monique attempted to sneak back out of the room, but Jocelyn spotted her. Jocelyn was actually glad that Monique came into the room and invited the distraction. She needed to come up for air.

"Monique, can I have a glass of water? You know what. I will go get it myself. I know where it is." Jocelyn knew she was rambling but couldn't help it.

Monique asked Terrell if he wanted anything. He just looked at Jocelyn and then back at Monique before telling Monique he was all set.

In the kitchen Monique cornered Jocelyn.

"Well J, what's up?" Monique wanted all the details.

"Nothing. We're just getting to know each other. Why are you looking at me like that?" Jocelyn answered.

Jocelyn knew she was already falling for Terrell or at least she felt like she was.

Monique smiled from ear to ear. "I just know I have a girlfriend named Jocelyn who looks and sounds a lot like you but who doesn't kiss guys on the first date. She believes it gets in the way of the "getting to know the person" process. But that couldn't be you because I just saw you kissing Terrell on the couch." Monique was laughing loudly at this point and Jocelyn had nothing to say.

Jocelyn took her glass of water and walked back to the living room. Terrell looked up the minute he heard footsteps. "I thought you left. Climbed out a window or something."

"Why would you think that?" Jocelyn asked. "I was bombarded by a nosy friend but definitely not thinking of escaping." Then she did something that even surprised her: she bent over and kissed Terrell. She shocked herself but it felt right. When they came up for air again Michael was standing over them again.

Michael asked Terrell if he wanted to go play basketball. He told Terrell that he would be leaving in about a half-hour and would come down and check to see if he wanted to go. Michael still had the same unimpressed look on his face. He smiled a coy smile at Jocelyn before leaving the room. Once again, Michael's actions brought Jocelyn and Terrell to laughter. They looked each other in the eyes and went back to doing what they had been doing for most of the afternoon, kissing.

Michael returned in a half-hour just as he said he would. "Are you going, man?" Michael inquired. "I'll swing you by your house to change clothes."

To Jocelyn's disappointment Terrell answered. "OK. Just let me say good-bye and we can be out. Where's your girlfriend?"

"Man, I don't know. I thought she would be snooping behind one of the doors or something, trying to see what you two were up to, but she's not," Michael answered and then asked Terrell why.

"I wanted to thank her for her hospitality and introducing me to Jocelyn," Terrell told him while still looking around for Monique.

"Alright man, do your thing. I'll be in the car. Don't take too long. If you see Monique, tell her I'll be back later." Mike said before heading down the stairs.

Terrell turned to Jocelyn and smiled. "Am I going to talk to you later?"

"I hope so." Jocelyn replied smiling back at Terrell although she was disappointed that he was leaving.

"I will definitely call you. Tell Monique I said good-bye and thanks. What time will you be home?" Terrell asked as he reached the stairs. When he looked back at Jocelyn, he couldn't help himself. He came back across the room and began kissing her again.

"I have to go right?" Terrell spoke first.

"Yeah," Jocelyn answered. "Michael and basketball are waiting for you."

Monique came in just as Terrell began to walk off again. He gave her a big tight hug, kissed her on the cheek, and thanked her for everything. He also told her that Mike said he would be back later. Monique smiled and rubbed Terrell on the head before he started down the stairs.

"Looks like a very happy man." Monique started as she heard the door shut. "Can't imagine why he is so happy. Oh yeah, he spent the afternoon making out with my friend. So do you like him?" Monique finished with a grin.

"Yeah, I like him. I like him a lot. I am just so drawn to him." Jocelyn admitted.

Monique couldn't stop smiling. She asked Jocelyn for details. What type of kisser was Terrell? Was she going to see him again? The question Monique really wanted an answer to was if she had done well. Jocelyn wasn't the type to let anyone hook her up. She had a very particular taste and only she could spot it.

Jocelyn affirmed that Monique had done well. She told Monique he was not her type, but she liked him and would try to make it work. Monique was so happy for Jocelyn.

"You deserve someone in your life. You work hard and go to school and everything. You are a good person and I know you say you don't need anyone in your life, but I think it will do you good."

"Thanks Monique. I don't need a man, but I don't mind having one. But he is not my man yet." Jocelyn answered.

"Always the pessimist. You are going to be just fine. I can tell he likes you too." Monique told Jocelyn through her smile.

Monique left the kitchen to get the glasses from the living room. When she returned Jocelyn was somewhere other than the kitchen.

"What are you thinking about? Terrell?" Monique startled Jocelyn.

"No! I'm just thinking." Jocelyn shot back.

"About Terrell? Naw, I'm joking. What are you thinking about?" Monique asked again.

"About life and everything. Just thinking in general. Don't worry. I like him." Jocelyn reassured Monique.

After they finished cleaning up, Jocelyn told Monique she was going to run some errands and pick up dinner somewhere. Monique invited her to stay and have dinner, but Jocelyn declined saying she had some studying to do. Monique looked at her like she really wanted her to stay but she said OK and walked Jocelyn to the front door. They talked for another hour in the doorway before Jocelyn hugged Monique and walked off.

Chapter 2

That night Jocelyn was studying—or at least she was trying to. Visions of Terrell and their encounter kept popping into her mind. She was smiling but this was not a good thing. She really needed to get her mind focused on her studies. She couldn't believe this person she had just met was occupying her mind this way and wondered what was going on. She gave up and was just sitting at her desk smiling when her phone rang.

"Hello," Jocelyn answered.

Terrell said hello back.

"How was the rest of your day?" He asked.

"Fine. I spent time with Monique and then I did some shopping and I just got through studying." Jocelyn wondered why she told him all of that and laughed out loud.

"What's so funny?" Terrell asked. "It couldn't be anything I said. I haven't said anything yet."

"I was just wondering why I mapped my afternoon out for you. I could have just told you that it was good." Jocelyn said.

"Yeah, you could have, but I'm glad you told me everything. It made me feel like you wanted to share with me." Terrell's answer made Jocelyn smile.

Jocelyn continued, "So how was basketball and male bonding?"

"Male bonding? Is that anything like the bonding you and

Monique had going on after we left? Is that what you are inquiring about?" he asked.

"No. I mean the cursing, battering, and jokes you guys' call playing basketball," Jocelyn answered quickly.

Terrell had to laugh because that was a lot of what went on when the guys got together to play basketball. "Oh that. Yeah, it was great," he answered through his laughter.

They talked for hours about everything and realized they had a lot in common. Jocelyn laughed at almost everything Terrell said. Some of the things were not meant to be funny but Terrell didn't care. He loved hearing her laugh. Jocelyn looked at the clock and realized that it was two thirty in the morning. She hated to hang up, but she had a class in the morning. It was bad enough that she hadn't completed her reading.

"I have to say good night," Jocelyn started. "I had such a good time talking to you. I could talk to you forever."

She shocked herself again. She's a never been so open with any man, especially not one she'd met only hours before.

"I'm glad to hear that, because I plan to talk to you forever." Terrell answered and said good night.

Jocelyn couldn't believe this. What was happening to her and why was it happening so fast? First, she kissed him, and now she was telling him everything. She thought to herself that she would have to start checking her swing, as they say in baseball. She couldn't believe it. She felt so sprung so early in the relationship.

Naw, she is not sprung, she thought before jumping into the shower. She also wondered why she couldn't wipe the silly grin off her face. She buried her face into her hands in the shower while she replayed the day in her head. She had never felt this way before and it was confusing her. She liked it though, and hoped she would always feel like this.

The honeymoon period for Jocelyn and Terrell ended as quickly as it started. Terrell all but stopped calling after they talked for a little more than a month. When Terrell did call, the phone calls were short and Jocelyn wondered what had changed. At first, she thought it was her imagination so she didn't question it. When she spoke to Monique, she was told that it is odd he isn't calling her.

Monique's second question was "Did you sleep with him?"

Jocelyn was horrified by Monique's question. She began to wonder if sex had something to do with Terrell's distance. She told Monique she would not dignify her question with an answer and attempted to rush her off the phone. Monique had more questions.

"Damn! Has he even tried to sleep with you?" Monique asked.

"Why are you asking me this?" Jocelyn asked.

Monique explained to Jocelyn that she believes sex confuses things, especially when it happens at the beginning of a relationship. She told Jocelyn to hold and dialed Terrell's number. Jocelyn was shocked when Terrell answered. She almost hung up.

Monique started off by asking what's up and then tore into Terrell.

"So, what's with you? Why haven't you been answering my girl's phone calls?" Monique asked.

"What do you mean?" Terrell asked her. "Is that what she told you?"

"So, you mean to tell me you have been returning her calls and everything is fine? I didn't hook you up with my girl for you to disrespect her," Monique sternly stated.

Terrell sucked his teeth but didn't respond to Monique's inquiry. There was a moment of silence before he began speaking. "Next time your girl has a problem with me, tell her to call me herself."

Jocelyn tried to hold it back, but she couldn't. "First of all, I didn't know she was calling you. Also, you say I should call you myself, but I have been calling you and you aren't returning my phone calls."

What Terrell said next totally shocked Jocelyn and Monique. "You know what? I don't need this. I am too old for the games. We should just forget the whole thing."

"What do you mean?" Jocelyn hesitantly asked.

"I don't want to do this anymore," Terrell answered.

He said his peace and hung up the phone before Jocelyn or Monique could respond.

Monique spoke first. "I'm sorry, Joce. I don't know what his problem is, but you definitely don't need that. Better sooner than later."

"What just happened?" Jocelyn responded. She had no idea what caused Terrell's attitude.

"He's being a jerk. Don't even think about him anymore. I can't believe the nerve of him," Monique answered. "Hey, do you want to go to the park later and hang out? It's been a while since I have seen you."

Jocelyn said, "Sure." Right away she wondered why. She didn't want to go to the park and thought for sure Terrell would be there. "Actually, I don't want to go. What if Terrell is there?"

"Ignore him. C'mon Joce. I know you are not going to let this man run you out of a park you have been going to all your life," Monique retorted. Jocelyn thought about it, and they agreed to meet in about an hour at the park.

Sure enough, Terrell was at the park when they arrived. He watched them as they walked through the crowd and took seats on the bleachers. One of the guys on the court yelled at Terrell to get his attention. What he yelled shocked Jocelyn, "Man, we told you about that stuck up girl. She's out of your league. Come on. Play ball or get off the court."

Jocelyn looked at Monique and asked, "Who is that? He is talking like he knows me."

"That's David. He went to high school with us. You really don't know him?" Monique inquired.

"No. I don't know him or what his problem is," Jocelyn responded angrily. She got up to leave but Monique pulled her back down.

"Don't let them get to you," Monique told her.

They stayed at the park for most of the afternoon and to both of their surprise, Terrell came over to say hi. Jocelyn held her tongue but wanted to curse him for the way he acted on the phone. She smiled and nodded and kept walking. Monique looked back to see how Terrell responded to Jocelyn's acknowledgement. He was standing there with a half smirk, half frown on his face.

"Yo, Joce. He's still standing there looking all pitiful," Monique said as they were leaving the park.

"I got him. I didn't do anything to him," Jocelyn responded. "Did he actually think I would talk to him after the way he talked to me?"

Monique just looked at Jocelyn. "Of course, Terrell thought you should talk to him. He probably doesn't think he did anything wrong."

"Well, he can forget it," Jocelyn stated bluntly. "And that other guy, I should go give him a piece of my mind. He don't know me."

Jocelyn stopped walking and contemplated going back to confront this David person. How dare he call her stuck up? She turned to Monique, "Do you think I am stuck up?"

The question threw Monique totally off guard. "What? No. If I thought you were stuck up, I wouldn't even mess with you."

"Did the guys in high school think I was stuck up?" Jocelyn continued her questioning.

Monique glanced at Jocelyn before she answered. "Some of them. But they don't know what they are talking about."

"Why would they think that? They never tried to get to know me." Jocelyn was stunned by Monique's words.

"They didn't think they could get to know you," Monique answered casually. "I know a couple of guys who wanted to talk to you but said they didn't think they could."

"How does that equal me being stuck up?" Jocelyn questioned.

"It doesn't, but when word got around it made it seem like you were unapproachable, and you know your brother was blocking guys from talking to you," Monique said. She continued to look at Jocelyn, trying to gauge her attitude. "I wouldn't even worry about it. You're in college, doing your thing. Let them talk. It shouldn't even bother you."

"It bothers me because they are feeding it to Terrell, and it is not true." Jocelyn whined.

═══

That night, Jocelyn called Terrell and to her surprise he answered on the first ring.

"Hey Jocelyn. I saw you at the park today. Why didn't you speak?"

Jocelyn was confused. Was this his way of trying to make small talk? "I saw you too." She thought she would play along with Terrell, but she couldn't hold it in anymore. "So, what else have those guys been telling you?"

"What guys?" Terrell asked.

"The one who called me stuck up and any others who may have had something to say," Jocelyn answered quickly.

"Oh, I don't listen to them. I don't even know them like that," Terrell responded.

"OK. I just want to let you know I don't either and they don't know me or anything about me." Jocelyn tried to keep the frustration out of her voice, but she knew it was there. The whole situation was bothering her. "So, if it isn't them, what is your problem?"

"I don't have a problem." Terrell's voice was showing frustration now.

"So why did you act the way you did when we were on the phone with Monique?" Jocelyn asked.

"Because I didn't like getting double teamed," He answered.

"We weren't double teaming you," Jocelyn responded. She thought about it for a while and saw why he could get that impression. "I'm sorry but I wasn't trying to double team you. I was just curious why things changed between us."

"What changed?" He asked. He was serious too.

Jocelyn told Terrell that since he didn't always call her back when she called him, she thought he was pulling away from her. He told her that wasn't the case. He just had a lot of things he needed to do and sometimes when he thought about calling, it was late and he didn't want to wake her knowing she had classes in the morning.

Jocelyn felt relieved. They continued to talk and made plans for the weekend. They also talked about listening to what other people had to say and promised to always talk to each other if they heard something they wanted to question the other about. It was three o'clock in the morning when they hung up. Jocelyn went to sleep with a smile. She liked Terrell and wanted things to work out find Terrell now.

"When you weren't around," Monique answered, shocking Jocelyn.

"Ouch. I'm sorry. You know you could have called me if you needed anything. I am never too busy for you."

"You were too busy to call me." Monique shot back. "You know what, forget about it. You have your own problems. That's why you are calling now."

"What?" Jocelyn was shocked at what Monique said.

"What is going on with you and Terrell?" Monique continued. "What did he do now?"

"He didn't do anything," Jocelyn answered. That was actually the truth. Terrell didn't do anything.

"So, everything is good between you?" Monique asked.

"Yes. He was just over here a while ago," Jocelyn answered. "Why are you acting like that is the only reason I would call you?"

"Because I haven't heard from you," Monique answered.

Jocelyn continued with the lie. She knew Monique knew her well enough to know she was lying, but she didn't want Monique to be right.

"So, what have you been up to?" Jocelyn asked.

"Nothing, working." Monique's answer was an exasperated one, meaning she didn't want to continue the conversation. "Well, it was nice hearing from you. Don't be a stranger. Tell Terrell I said hello when you see him."

Jocelyn knew she was on to her, but she was not going to give Monique the satisfaction. "You too. We have to get together and go out or something."

up and putting them on. When he finished, he didn't even look back at Jocelyn. He just left. She sat on the bed and put her head in her hands. She had no idea what happened or why she responded like that to Terrell. She thought about calling him but realized he probably wouldn't answer her call.

Jocelyn then thought she should go after him. She tried to think of where he would go but had no idea. She thought about calling Monique but didn't want to hear what she would have to say about the situation. She would have definitely had something to say about Jocelyn even talking to Terrell again.

Against her better judgment she called Monique.

"Hey girl," Jocelyn responded when Monique answered.

"Hey stranger. Where have you been?"

"I've been around, in school and chilling with Terrell." Jocelyn thought getting it out at the beginning was best in this case.

"Terrell? How is he doing?" Monique asked. Jocelyn was wondering if that was all that she wanted to say. Almost on queue Monique went on, "So how long have you two been talking?"

"A few months now. Actually, we started talking again after the incident in the park," Jocelyn answered.

Monique said, "OK."

It was a sarcastic ok, but Jocelyn didn't respond to it. She wasn't going to press the issue or ask what the problem was, so she changed the subject.

"So how is Michael?"

"We broke up." Monique answered quickly and with a noticeable attitude.

"When?" Jocelyn asked. Knowing there is no way she would

he responded. "I didn't mean anything by it. Haven't you ever been in love?"

"How many people have you been in love with?" Jocelyn snapped.

"Is that really the question you wanted to ask me?" Terrell snapped back. "Or did you mean to ask how many people I have slept with?"

"Both." Jocelyn was really curious now.

"I have never been in love before you, and I have slept with 3 girls," he answered matter-of-factly.

Jocelyn couldn't talk or move. She didn't know what shocked her more was the fact he said he is in love with her, or the fact that he has slept with three girls he didn't love. She was a little sorry she asked but she didn't stop.

"So how many of those girls did you tell you loved them?"

"What?" Terrell was shocked. This is not the way things were supposed to be going right now.

"How many?" Jocelyn repeated. She knew he heard her.

"None. One. I don't know." His annoyance was written all over his face. "Are you saying I told them I loved them to get them to sleep with me?"

"Did you?" Jocelyn asked.

"I don't need this. When you want to talk to me, you know where to find me." Terrell picked up his clothes off the floor.

"So, you'd rather leave than answer my question?" Jocelyn asked. She couldn't understand it herself. Why was she picking a fight with him?

Terrell didn't answer Jocelyn. He continued picking his things

Chapter 3

Things went well for a few months. Jocelyn and Terrell spent most of their free time together as well as time that wasn't actually free. One day, they were in Jocelyn's house and things started getting a little hot for Jocelyn's comfort. They were fooling around, and clothes started coming off. They had been naked around each other before—they'd even slept in the same bed in the nude.

Terrell was like a man on a mission. It had been six months since they first met, and he thought it was time for them to take the relationship to the next level. He knew he loved her, and she loved him, and to him it was the natural next step. He kissed her heavily, not giving her the opportunity to talk or think. Little did he know Jocelyn was thinking about what was happening and didn't know if she was ready.

They continued to make out. He was rubbing her and touching her, thinking it was going well and it was going to happen when Jocelyn stopped him.

"What's wrong baby?" Terrell asked.

"I can't do--" Jocelyn responded. She actually shocked herself with her answer and then changed it. "I mean I have never..." She couldn't finish her sentences.

"Never?" Terrell asked. "Why?"

"What do you mean, why?" Jocelyn asked. "What kind of question is that?"

"I don't know. Most of the people I know have already had sex,

That's how their conversation ended. Jocelyn was at a loss for words when she hung up with Monique. She didn't even realize she hadn't been speaking to Monique. Maybe it's good things didn't work out with Terrell. She would never neglect her friends because of a man. Friends are forever but men come and go. She was at a crossroad. She didn't know if she wanted to call him now, but the damage was already done with Monique.

Jocelyn wouldn't have to call Terrell. He called her. She was both relieved and confused. Terrell answered her greeting with "How are you?"

"I'm ok. I'm sorry!" Jocelyn exclaimed.

"I am too," he responded. "I don't want to seem like I am pressuring you. You mean so much more to me than having sex. I'll wait for you."

"Don't," Jocelyn countered. She didn't know where that came from, but it was too late to take it back.

"What?" Terrell asked.

"Don't wait for me. I figured out that I need to rebalance my focus. I have let a lot of things go in the past few months and I need to reconnect." Yeah, it made sense, but it was not what she really felt.

"What are you saying?" Terrell asked.

"I'm saying we need to take a break." Jocelyn was answering but she couldn't connect the words that were coming out of her mouth.

"Are you sure? I told you I would not pressure you to have sex." His tone was almost desperate.

"Yeah, I'm sure. I'm sorry," Jocelyn answered.

"OK, I'll give you your time, space, whatever it is you need. Let me know when you are ready." Terrell's voice was low and soft. Jocelyn went to respond but he had hung up the phone.

Jocelyn felt like a jerk. She couldn't believe she did that. She thought about his last statement and how he sounded. She wondered what he meant by "let him know when she is ready." She was ready. She just didn't think he was the one she needed to be with at this point in her life.

Chapter 4

Jocelyn did the things she said she was going to do. She got her focus back in school and even changed her major to pre-law. She also reconnected with her friends and family. She was getting ready to go out with Monique. Monique and Michael still weren't talking, but Monique didn't want to believe it was over. She heard rumors of him having a girlfriend but refused to believe them, saying the girl was only a chick on the side.

Jocelyn tried to keep her responses to Monique's rants to a minimum, she didn't want to say anything that would set Monique off. She was surprised Monique had agreed to go out. Monique typically didn't do much of anything but go to work and come home. She seemed relieved when Jocelyn came back around. Jocelyn told her she was right, and things were not good between her and Terrell, so she broke it off. After a couple of sideways "I told you so" looks, all was forgiven.

At the club, Monique seemed out of place until a guy came up and asked her to dance. She took off with him and they danced for a long time. When they finished dancing, she didn't come back to where Jocelyn was. She went with the guy to the other side of the club. Jocelyn didn't want to seem like she was crowding them, so she didn't go over. There were no other familiar faces in the place so now she was the one who felt out of place.

That's when it happened. He walked right up to her like nothing ever happened between them.

"How have you been?" Terrell asked. He looked good. He asked her to dance. Jocelyn attempted to say no but she said yes instead. She started to wonder why she always said the opposite of what she felt with this guy. He grabbed her hand and led her to the floor. They danced for a few songs before Monique came over.

"You haven't learned?" Monique asked as she stared Terrell down.

"What is your problem?" Terrell asked.

"What is your problem?" Monique snapped back at Terrell. "Why don't you leave her alone?"

Terrell turned to Jocelyn. "Is that what you want?"

"I wanted it when I said it, but I am not so sure anymore," Jocelyn answered. Her answer came as a surprise to all of them.

"Well don't let me interrupt your reunion." Monique stormed off, leaving them on the floor.

Jocelyn took off after Monique. She was curious to find out what her attitude was about.

"What was that all about?" Jocelyn asked when she caught up with Monique.

"Why do you keep letting this guy hurt you?" she asked.

"He didn't hurt me. I broke it off with him," Jocelyn responded.

"Why? If he is so perfect, why would you break up with him?" Monique asked the questions Jocelyn had in her mind for the longest time.

"I don't know." Jocelyn answered.

"You do know," Monique shot back.

Monique walked off and went over to the guy she was dancing with. A couple of minutes later she left with him. Jocelyn just watched Monique leave, not remembering she came with Monique. When she remembered she frantically looked for Terrell. He was standing by the bar talking to a girl but when he saw Jocelyn, he tapped the girl on the shoulder and walked toward Jocelyn.

Jocelyn explained what happened with Monique and she needed a ride home. To her surprise Terrell agreed to take her. He went back to the girl he was talking to and said goodbye before leading Jocelyn out of the club.

"Who is that?" Jocelyn asked.

"Oh no you don't. You have no right to ask me anything about anyone," He replied, sounding agitated.

"I was just curious. I wasn't looking for an argument," Jocelyn quietly responded.

Terrell looked over at Jocelyn for what seemed like a long time. He then apologized for snapping at her, telling her he doesn't know how to take her curiosity.

He continued by asking, "How is everything? How is school, life, etc.?"

Jocelyn still felt his attitude and called him on it. "What's with the attitude?"

He apologized and didn't say anything else for a long time.

"You know I love you?" Terrell asked, breaking the silence.

Jocelyn looked at him. She couldn't believe he would just spring something like that on her. Why now?

"You do?" Jocelyn asked. "Why?"

"I can't call it," he answered with a grin. Then he got serious. "I can't get you out of my mind. I guess I just do. Don't worry. I don't expect you to return the love. I know you don't love me."

"How can you assume I don't love you?" Jocelyn quickly asked in defense. She was still surprised at him saying she didn't love him but didn't know how to respond to it. His assumption threw her for a loop, but she still didn't tell him that she did.

"Did you love me?" Terrell asked.

"Yes," answered Jocelyn.

Then he asked, "Do you love me?"

Jocelyn remained quiet. She does love him, but she didn't feel it made any difference at this point.

"So why can't we make it work?" He responded. "Why won't you be with me?"

"I don't know. I am sorry about what happened before. I didn't mean to assume you were trying to take advantage of me." Jocelyn answered his questions.

They sat in silence for the rest of the drive. When Terrell stopped the car in front of Jocelyn's house, he turned and stared at her. She didn't make a move to get out of the car. He reached over, grabbed her face, and kissed her. She didn't pull away. Part of her wanted to but she didn't. It felt like the first time they kissed—butterflies fluttered deep in her stomach. No way, she thought, but she felt them.

They continued to kiss in the car for what seemed like hours. She couldn't catch her breath. Then Terrell suddenly backed off and apologized. Jocelyn looked him in his eyes and could see the pain in them. She reached out to his face and rubbed her hand up and down the side of it. "You don't have to apologize unless you didn't mean it."

"Oh, I meant it," Terrell said. "I just didn't want you to think I was taking advantage of the situation."

Terrell decided it was time to call it a night. He asked Jocelyn if he could call her in the morning. She agreed to him calling, saying that they needed to talk. This time she did get out of the car. She looked back at the car the whole time as she walked toward her parents' house. She couldn't believe she was going there with Terrell again. Terrell stayed parked in front of her house. until she got inside.

The next day Terrell didn't call, he came over to Jocelyn's parents' house. Jocelyn's mother answered the door. She didn't know how to respond to Terrell being there because the last she heard things were over between the two of them. She told him to come in and she would see if Jocelyn was there or not, explaining that she hadn't seen her all morning.

Mrs. McCrary got to Jocelyn's room and knocked on the door. Jocelyn didn't answer at first, so she was ready to walk away and tell Terrell that she wasn't home when she heard Jocelyn call, "Who is it?"

"Let me in, sweetheart," Mrs. McCrary responded quietly.

Jocelyn complied. After opening the door, she looked at Jocelyn for a second, trying to read her face. For some reason she looked sad.

"What's wrong honey?" Her mother asked.

"Nothing to worry about," Jocelyn responded, putting on a fake smile for her mother. A smile her mother saw right through.

"Did Terrell do something Joce?" Her mother asked, still not telling Jocelyn he was downstairs. If he did something she would gladly have her husband escort him out the house.

"He told me he loves me," Jocelyn answered. "I feel the same, but for some reason he thought I didn't love him."

Her mother stared at her for a couple of minutes, forgetting why she came into the room in the first place. She wondered why Jocelyn wasn't telling Terrell she loved him. Just as she was about to ask Jocelyn why, her father knocked on the door. Jocelyn's father poked his head in and asked if anyone knew the young man sitting on the couch. Jocelyn's mother looked up and said, "Oh yeah. Terrell is downstairs. That is why I came up here. Sorry, I got sidetracked."

"Downstairs?" Jocelyn's confusion was evident. "He said he was going to call me."

Jocelyn looked around the room for something to put on. She ran to the mirror to look at her face and hair. After making sure everything was in order, she followed her parents downstairs. Mr. McCrary went over first and introduced himself to Terrell. They shook hands and Mr. McCrary asked him a couple of questions before leading his wife out of the living room, leaving Terrell and Jocelyn to talk.

Jocelyn spoke first after her parents left the room. "What are you doing here? You were supposed to call."

"I know, but I wanted to see you and talk to you in person, and I didn't want to give you the opportunity to say no," Terrell said.

Jocelyn looked at Terrell and thought that she probably would have said no to meeting him to talk.

"Do you want me to go?" Terrell's words snapped Jocelyn out of her thought.

"No," she answered. "I do not want you to go."

They talked for a couple of hours. The whole time Terrell held Jocelyn in his arms, they discussed what they wanted out of their relationship and how they felt about each other.

Terrell made Jocelyn aware of the fact that he needed more time and effort from her. He understood that she had school and other obligations, but he wanted to be a priority also. She told him that he can't listen to the people outside their relationship and made Terrell aware she would need time to devote to her studies.

They realized that they do love each other, and it would take more of an effort than they both were making. At the end of the conversation, they decided they would give it another try. She told him that she felt like she got so lost in their relationship the last time that she wasn't devoting enough time to her studies. Terrell said he was ok with that as long as she let him know that is what it is, so he doesn't think he did something wrong.

They made plans to go out for dinner that night. Terrell wanted to go out right then and there, but Jocelyn had a couple of things she needed to do. She walked him to his car and gave him a kiss. She tried to walk away but he grabbed her by the waist and held her close to him, softly kissing her on the forehead. Then he raised her head by her chin and kissed her lips. Jocelyn felt chills up and down her body.

She could have stayed like that forever but looked around and saw her father looking out the door. She gave Terrell one more kiss before she broke free and walked away. Terrell watched her walk away and enter her parents' house before he got in his car and drove off.

She expected her parents to question her when she got back into the house, but they didn't. She went up to her room and found something to wear on their date. She thought about the conversation she had with Terrell and vowed to try harder. She did love him and wanted their relationship to work

Chapter 5

Everything went well in their relationship for the next three years. They saw each other when Jocelyn came home from school on weekends and holidays and spoke to each other almost every night unless Jocelyn had a lot of studying to do. Terrell even came to visit her at school on the weekends she couldn't make it home. At least as far as Jocelyn was concerned, their relationship was going okay. She didn't hear any complaints from Terrell.

The closer she got to graduating from college, the more arguments and fights they got into. He wanted more time than Jocelyn had to give and felt like they were at a stalemate. It got to the point that Jocelyn didn't talk to Terrell for the whole month before she was to graduate because she wanted to focus on her finals without arguing. When she did call him, he seemed like everything was ok. She thought he understood that it was a crucial time and that she needed more time for her studies. So Jocelyn was thrown for a loop what happened next.

Jocelyn invited Terrell to go to a formal for graduating seniors. He agreed to take her and assured her he had a suit to wear. She started to call Terrell at three o'clock when she was leaving the campus. She got home from the salon around four thirty, but still hadn't heard anything from Terrell. She called when she got to her parents' house to make sure Terrell knew that she was there and not at school, thinking maybe they had their wires crossed.

She waited and waited for Terrell to call or to show up, but he didn't. She called his house, no answer. She called his cell phone again, no answer. Finally, Jocelyn decided that she was going to the formal without him. She wasn't going to let him ruin her night.

Jocelyn went to the formal, but after an hour of people asking her where her boyfriend was and her not having an answer or any fun, she left. In the car ride home she felt like crying but tried to hold it in. She couldn't believe he stood her up, knowing how important this time was to her.

She made it to the driveway before the tears came streaming down her eyes. She wanted to get it all out before she went into her parents' house because she knew they would have questions. She banged on the steering wheel screaming and wondering why Terrell did this to her.

Jocelyn attempted to call Terrell again when she got into the house but was met with the same results: no answer. Jocelyn decided she wasn't going to call him anymore. She didn't even want to hear any excuse he could possibly give for doing this to her. She thought that he should have had the decency to tell her he didn't want to go, or that things were over between them. She picked up the phone and relayed that on his voicemail and went back to her original plan of not calling anymore.

Graduation came and passed, and Jocelyn still hadn't heard from Terrell. This left her in a somber mood through all the activities and everyone seemed to notice. Her mother was the first person to comment on it.

"Where is Terrell?" She asked Jocelyn at dinner after the ceremony.

"I don't know, Mama," Jocelyn answered. She hoped no one would say anything to her about it because she didn't want to cry. "I called him, but he hasn't returned my calls."

"Why? I didn't know you guys were having problems." Jocelyn

wished her mother would just let it go but she knew her better than that.

"I didn't either. Maybe he'll come around," Jocelyn answered.

Jocelyn wasn't sure he would or if she even wanted him to. She looked around the table to see if anyone else was picking up on her mood. She saw her father looking at her, but she smiled him away. At least she thought she did. If he had anything to say, he didn't. He just raised his glass and toasted her.

"To my beautiful, smart daughter. Congratulations," Jocelyn's dad said with his head and his glass held high. "I am so proud of you."

When Jocelyn looked at him to thank him, he winked at her. It was always his little way of letting her know he knew something, and it usually made her feel better. This time it made her let all the tears she held back flow. At least she had a reason now. Her mother looked over at her knowingly, but everyone else appeared to think she was just overwhelmed by her father's toast. They continued dinner in silence and the silence continued during the ride home.

When they got home, everyone gave her a kiss and headed their separate ways. Jocelyn went to her bedroom, sat down on her bed, and began to think. Before she knew what she was doing she picked up the phone and dialed Terrell's number. To her surprise he answered.

"Where have you been?" Jocelyn asked, trying to hold back the tears. Her voice was cracking so she knew she wasn't fooling him.

"What? I don't have to tell you where I have been," He answered.

"Yes, you do. You promised to take me to the dance the other night and you didn't show up." Jocelyn continued, although what she really wanted to do was hang up the phone. "You stood me up. Why couldn't you be there during one of the most important times of my life?"

"Because it wouldn't have been real. I couldn't just be there for you knowing that the end is near," Terrell answered. "Not as in the sense that I'm not happy for you, because I am happy for you. I know you worked hard."

Jocelyn was really confused now, "End? What? What are you talking about?"

"The end of our relationship," Terrell said. "I thought about it, and I can't go on acting like everything is all good. You are going to law school and it is only going to get worse, so I am bailing out now."

Jocelyn was taken aback by Terrell's revelation. They have never talked about ending their relationship. Even when things were bad, she didn't think ending it was an option. She began crying but quickly composed herself.

"Bail out, huh? You are a coward. Instead of telling me to my face you ignored me, stood me up, and just totally disregarded how I may feel about it!" Jocelyn screamed. She knew she was screaming but she really didn't care at this point. "I can't believe you would do this to me. I thought you loved me."

"I do love you. That is why it hurts me to not have all of you. Maybe you can't understand because you have all of me. Anytime you call, I'm there. Anything you want, I try to oblige. But when I call it's 'I have to study', or 'I am busy but maybe later'. I want someone who is going to be there for me."

Terrell got out everything he had been feeling for a long time but had held in, and it threw Jocelyn for a loop. She wanted to say something but couldn't find the words. She still thought he should have been honest with her or met with her and talked it out instead of choosing to handle it in a childish manner. She decided not to fight anymore and to just let him go. She hung the phone up silently. No goodbye. No nothing. She didn't even know if he knew she hung it up, but she didn't care at that point.

Terrell called her right back. Yep, he realized she had hung up. She let it go to her voice mail. He told her he loved her and always would. He also said he hoped one day she would understand what he was talking about. He apologized for missing her graduation and congratulated her before he hung up. That was that... until they saw each other about a year ago.

Chapter 6

Jocelyn was walking in the mall when she saw him. She wasn't sure it was Terrell, so she kept walking. Terrell was sure he was looking at Jocelyn and came right up to her.

"So, you were just going to walk past me, no hello, no nothing?" Terrell asked.

"I didn't realize it was you," she answered. "I thought it looked like you, but I wasn't sure. I didn't want to embarrass myself, so I didn't come over."

His facial expression made Jocelyn believe he didn't believe her. Jocelyn frankly didn't care what he believed.

"How have you been?" he asked, changing the subject.

Jocelyn answered, "Good, how about you?"

He answered that he was doing fine, informed Jocelyn that he had a new job and was promoted a few months ago.

With a smile he said, "I finally got off my ass and got some initiative."

Jocelyn blushed. "I only said that once out of anger. I didn't mean it, although I always thought you could do more." She'd felt it then but had only said it to him because she was angry that he didn't understand her being into her studies.

"I'm glad to hear it," Jocelyn said, trying not to get too sucked into his life. "Anything else new with you?" She asked.

"As a matter of fact, I have a son. He is almost three. I forgot I haven't seen you in a long time. What's it been? About 10 years?" He added, "His mother and I are no longer together. It wasn't meant to be, she is getting married this summer."

Jocelyn thought to herself he was giving her too much information but answered, "A son, wow. Congratulations."

Terrell asked if she had any children, a husband, or a boyfriend. When Jocelyn told him no, he just stared at her until she asked, "What are you staring at?"

He told her, "I was just wondering why such a beautiful person is still single."

This made Jocelyn blush again, but she was not ready to let her guard down where Terrell was concerned. She knew it was over and had finally moved on. She coyly responded, "I just haven't met my match yet."

They talked for a while longer before Jocelyn told Terrell she had to go. She was meeting a friend for dinner and had to find an outfit, and she only had an hour to get home and get dressed. He asked if it was a date and Jocelyn just looked at him. He swore he wasn't trying to pry but the grin on his face said otherwise. He kissed her on her forehead and left her to find her outfit.

Jocelyn smiled as she continued shopping. She was in fact going on a date with a man she liked a lot. She'd met Jeff through her friend Karen, who she went to law school with. They had been talking for a few weeks. Jeff was the type of man Jocelyn had been looking for. He was educated, ambitious, and knew how to treat a woman. He was a lawyer at a well-known firm and was striving to be a partner.

His ambition was why it had taken them three weeks to finally link up and go out. He had been working on an important case but called her during any free time or time he felt like slacking. They talked about everything, including law. Jocelyn went to law school but decided she did not want to practice law. She kept up with the legal goings-on, and even helped Jeff out with a part of his case.

That was why they were going to dinner: to celebrate the end of the case and to finally spend some time alone. Dinner and dancing was what Jeff proposed for the night, so Jocelyn figured she would get a new outfit to mark the beginning of a new relationship.

In Macy's, Jocelyn grew tired of her search. She thought of all the outfits in her closet she had never worn and wondered if she could pair anything up. She scanned her closet in her mind and found something she thought would be appropriate. Then she thought about it—she had to pick something up because with her luck she would run into Terrell again. If she had no clothes in her hand, he would surely believe she lied to him to get away from him.

Jocelyn thought it through some more, and realized she didn't care what Terrell thought. She wasn't going to buy something to feed into this nonsense. She put down the shirt she had been considering.

As Jocelyn was walking back to her car, she saw Terrell again. This time, she ducked into a store and hoped he didn't see her. She did not have time for this right now. He either didn't see her, or he just didn't come into the store. When she was sure he had passed the store and had his back to where she was, she left the store and continued to her car.

When she reached her car, there was Terrell again. This time, there was a woman with him and they were getting into a car. The woman handed Terrell the keys before she got in on the passenger side. Jocelyn thought to herself, some things never change. Why should Terrell ever get his own, when there are women lined up to give it to him?

Oh well, she thought, Terrell was no longer her problem, and she wished him well.

So, what was this pit in her stomach?

Jocelyn turned her focus back to where it belonged: on Jeff and their date. She picked out an outfit in her mind she believed would be appropriate, but she didn't know where they were going. Jeff wanted to surprise her. She was beginning to get nervous about the date. It was the first one she had gone on in over a year and Jeff seemed so perfect.

Jeff picked her up at her house, on time. He had two dozen pink roses in his hand and looked amazing. Jeff stood at about six-foot-three with a mocha brown complexion. His lined-up goatee and beard made Jocelyn think back to when they'd met at Karen's party. She didn't remember him looking that good. Jocelyn had always loved to see men in suits and thought that was possibly what was making him look better to her. He'd had on jeans and a button-down shirt at the party.

"Wow, you look amazing," Jeff told Jocelyn before he presented her with the roses. She'd found a purple dress in her closet that still had the tags on it. She'd matched that with some black, strappy heels and had pulled her hair up into a messy bun-like creation. She had decided that less was more with the makeup, as she didn't want to look like she was trying too hard.

"Yeah, well you clean up well also counselor," Jocelyn said to Jeff with a smile. "Thanks for the flowers. I'll put them in some water and then we can go. Do you want anything?"

"No, I am fine thanks," Jeff answered.

He was looking around at Jocelyn's house and didn't even notice when Jocelyn came back into the room.

"Oops. I guess I got caught being nosy," said Jeff with a chuckle. "They say you can learn a lot about a person by their home."

"It's OK. Are you ready to go or do you want to snoop some more?" Jocelyn asked with a laugh. "Don't worry, you'll get the grand tour someday. I haven't done much to it since I inherited it from my grandmother."

In the car the conversation was just like it was on the phone. The conversation came easily. Jocelyn was so pleased with Jeff and loved having someone to talk to. She didn't have to explain everything to him like she did with Terrell. She thought to herself that would be the last time his name popped into her head for any reason that night.

Jeff pulled up in front of Bob's Bistro and let Jocelyn out. He told Jocelyn he was going to find a parking space and he would be right back. He told her she could go inside if she didn't feel comfortable standing outside. She told him she would wait outside and smiled as he drove off. Jocelyn was a little disappointed at his choice of restaurant. She felt she was overdressed for the BBQ restaurant scene. For that matter so was Jeff. It was cool though. She liked the food and there was a jazz band playing.

When they got in the restaurant and got a table, Jeff asked Jocelyn how she liked the place. She told him it was fine. She forgot Jeff wasn't from Boston originally until he told her he looked the restaurant up online and saw a brother owns it. "Gotta support the brothers." He told her, grinning from ear to ear.

After they finished eating, they stayed and listened to the jazz bands. The owner came over and asked if everything was satisfactory. Jocelyn was a little embarrassed when the owner called her by name— she'd let Jeff believe he had found the place.

The owner asked them if they were there on business. Jocelyn alerted the owner that they were there on a date. He said, "Oh, I'm sorry don't let me interrupt. You guys have a good night." He smiled, looked at Jeff one last time and went to the next table. As soon as he left Jeff looked at Jocelyn.

"So, you have been here before?" Jeff asked.

"Yes, several times," Jocelyn told him. "But I haven't been here in a long time."

"And you know the owner?" Jeff asked.

"I know him from here. He always checks in on his customers and gets their name and talks to them," Jocelyn answered.

She didn't know exactly what Jeff was asking but she didn't entertain him. She wasn't about to tell him she had been there with her ex-boyfriend.

After dinner they went to Scullers to listen to some more jazz. They walked into the place and Jeff turned to Jocelyn and asked, "So have you been here also?"

"I haven't. I've heard about it but never had the pleasure of coming here," Jocelyn answered.

Jeff looked pleased and Jocelyn just hoped no one recognized her and made her look like she comes here all the time.

Just as they were about to get on the dance floor Jocelyn ran into Terrell's mother. She feared his mother would say something, but she just asked Jocelyn how she was doing and who's the handsome young man. Jocelyn told her she had seen Terrell in the mall earlier with his girlfriend, and that the young man was her date. Terrell's mother just looked them up and down and went on her way. She was wondering who was with her son because he didn't have a girlfriend—at least not one she knew of. But she didn't tell Jocelyn that.

The rest of the night Jocelyn could feel Terrell's mother watching her. She and Jeff danced for what seemed like forever. At times they were the only couple on the floor dancing. Jeff felt good in her arms, and she didn't want to let him go. Jocelyn's feet began to hurt, and she needed to sit down. She alerted Jeff that she needed to sit, and he laughed.

"Sorry. It's been such a long time since I have been out. I just have all types of energy," Jeff told her.

"It's OK," Jocelyn responded. "I am enjoying myself also. We can go back out and dance more later."

"Do you want a drink?" Jeff asked. "I think I'll get a beer."

"Sure, I'll take a Cosmopolitan," Jocelyn answered.

Jeff laughed and asked if that was still the ladies drink of choice. Jocelyn nodded, "It's this lady's drink of choice." He told Jocelyn he would be right back and was off to the bar. Jocelyn was all smiles. She was really feeling a connection with Jeff. She felt the eyes on her, but she no longer cared. When Jeff returned with the drinks, he saw Jocelyn smiling and commented on it. He asked her if something happened while he was gone. Jocelyn shook her head and told Jeff, "You were here for every part of what is making me smile." She asked, "Do you feel the connection also."

Jeff answered, "Yes." Now they were both smiling.

On the way home there wasn't much conversation. Jocelyn began to grow nervous about showing her hand so soon. She didn't want to come off as easy or desperate. She wondered what Jeff was thinking. There was no better way to find out but to ask.

"What are you thinking?" Jocelyn asked Jeff.

Jeff laughed and then answered, "That I'm glad that case is over, and I got to go out with you." He looked over at Jocelyn and asked, "Did I look like I was thinking or are you a mind reader?"

"Nope, not a mind reader, just noting the silence," Jocelyn responded to his question.

"I was also trying to figure out a slick way to steal a kiss from you," said Jeff.

"Why steal?" Jocelyn asked.

"Because I honestly didn't think I would be able to get one this soon," Jeff said with a laugh in his voice. "Please put me out of my misery because it's been so long since I have dated. I couldn't think of a way to steal one."

"We'll see," Jocelyn responded, but laughed to let Jeff know she was joking.

She wanted him to kiss her.

"It's your turn. What are you thinking?" Jeff asked.

"Nothing," Jocelyn answered.

"That's not fair. I answered you and came off like a complete dork," Jeff retorted.

"You didn't sound like a dork. I thought it was cute," Jocelyn responded with a giggle.

"Great, now you're humoring me. Man, I must have sounded really corny. You know what?" Jeff stopped the car in the middle of the street.

He reached over, touched Jocelyn's face, and just went for it. He kissed Jocelyn and waited to be slapped or cursed out or something. He backed off for a minute to get a response. When he saw she didn't respond negatively he kissed her again. Jocelyn thought to herself, so much for playing it cool.

When they reached Jocelyn's house, Jeff walked her to her door. Jocelyn began joking with Jeff. "I would ask you up, but I don't trust you anymore."

Jeff gave Jocelyn a confused look. "What?"

"The way you took advantage of me in your car," Jocelyn said.

Jocelyn decided she had better start laughing because he looked scared.

"You scared me for a minute there." Jeff was confused. "Honestly if those kisses were unwanted, I apologize."

"No, they were not. I was joking with you. We're going to have to get you a sense of humor counselor."

Jeff looked at Jocelyn and smiled. "Noted. I'll pick one up in the morning. Thanks for the offer to come up but I have an early morning meeting," said Jeff.

"I didn't invite you up," Jocelyn answered him.

"Who needs a sense of humor now?" Jeff asked. Then he bent down and kissed Jocelyn again.

Jocelyn finally broke Jeff's grip. She told him she has an early morning also and although she would love to stand out here kissing him all night, she had to go. Jeff nodded and backed away, telling Jocelyn he had a wonderful time and he hoped to see her again. He asked Jocelyn to call him tomorrow and began walking toward his car.

Jocelyn wanted to let out a sigh of relief, a scream, or something. She decided she wouldn't just yet, because there were still plenty of things that could go wrong. She also decided she wouldn't tell Monique or anybody for the same reason. She was just so relieved to meet a man she could talk to and enjoy herself with. There was no sexual pressure, no trying to hold back, trying to be hard, just two people enjoying each other's company.

When Jocelyn walked into her house, she turned on her phone and saw she had messages. She was going to leave the messages until tomorrow but decided to listen to them in case it was something she needed for work in the morning.

The first message was from Terrell. Jocelyn wondered who gave him her phone number but decided she wouldn't persecute anyone for it. The message was a simple hello. He said how happy he was to see her in the mall that day and that she looked great. Message number two, also from Terrell. This message had a different tone and was left about twenty minutes ago.

"So, you're not home yet? Your date must have gone well? My

mother said she saw you. You could have told me you were going on a date. I wouldn't have said anything. It wouldn't have hurt me. Oh, the woman you saw me with is not my girlfriend. She is a co-worker, and she didn't feel like driving, so I drove. Anyway, I was just calling to say hi. Peace."

Jocelyn couldn't believe his mother ran home to tell him that she had seen her on a date. She also couldn't believe he had called to make sure she was home.

The phone rang while she was thinking about it. She looked at the phone number. It was Terrell. Her first thought was to pick it up and ask him where he got off checking up on her. Then she thought better of it and decided to let it go to voicemail. Let him think she was out all night if he wanted.

Monique called Jocelyn the next morning while she was at work. They talked for a while before Monique couldn't take it anymore.

"Where were you last night?" Monique asked. "I called around 12:30 to tell you Terrell was calling around asking for your phone number. Do you want him to have it?"

"Too late for that. Someone already gave it to him. He called three times last night," Jocelyn answered.

"It wasn't me. I got his number and told him I would give it to you. Do you want it?" Monique was keeping up the act.

"Nope got it off the caller ID. Any other time he would block his number," Jocelyn answered.

She was skeptical about what Monique was telling her and believed she probably did give it to him.

"What brought on his sudden interest in you?" Monique asked. "I thought he was long gone."

"I saw him in the mall yesterday. He came up to me, telling me how his life has changed. He didn't seem interested then," Jocelyn told Monique.

"So, are you going to talk to him? See what he wants?" Monique asked quickly.

Jocelyn thought to herself, this is the real reason Monique is calling, to get the tea and see if I had or if I was going to talk to Terrell.

"No, I don't think I will be doing that. I don't care what he wants," Jocelyn said.

She really didn't care, especially not after the night she'd had with Jeff. She thought of telling Monique but thought against it. Jocelyn told Monique she had to go because her boss wanted to meet with her. She told her she would talk to her later and hung up the phone before Monique got any more questions out.

Jocelyn began thinking about Jeff. He told her to call him, but she thought it was too soon. It was only eleven o'clock in the morning and she didn't want to sound too anxious. She decided to do some work and follow up on some of the phone calls that she needed to make.

Just before Jocelyn got up to go to lunch her phone rang. She wasn't going to answer it because she feared it was work-related and it would take time away from her lunch. She answered it anyway.

"What are you doing for lunch?" Jeff asked Jocelyn.

"I was headed out now. No plans. I'll probably walk around looking for food," Jocelyn answered.

"I'll be right there. I am already out. I have a meeting in a couple of hours and have to stop by Kinko's because my secretary is out. Oh, do you want to go to lunch with me?" Jeff said after realizing he was being presumptuous.

"Yes. I'll wait for you in front of the building. It is Exeter Plaza," Jocelyn told Jeff.

At lunch Jeff reminded Jocelyn he had a great time the night before. He apologized for calling so soon. He told her he wanted to give her time to think about whether he was someone she wanted to be with. He explained he was looking for much more than a fling at this point in his life and could see himself with her.

"Well, what do you think?" Jeff asked Jocelyn after his declaration.

"I think I would like to keep seeing you and see where it goes," Jocelyn answered.

Jocelyn didn't have a real answer to all of that. She knew she was not looking for a fling either. That had never been her style, but she thought Jeff was jumping the gun.

"I'm sorry I dropped all of this on you so soon. Like I said I haven't gone out with a woman in a long time, and I am talking too much," Jeff said, looking at the blank expression on Jocelyn's face.

"So, how is work going this morning?" Jeff continued, trying to change the subject.

"It's fine. I haven't had a productive morning though," Jocelyn answered.

"Really? Why?" Jeff asked.

"I am trying to get some grant proposals and contracts out and can't get in contact with the people I need to be in contact with," Jocelyn told him. It was that and the nerve of Terrell and whoever gave him her phone number. She was still scanning her mind, trying to figure out who would.

"Oh, sorry to hear that. I hope you will be able to reach them this afternoon," Jeff responded.

Jeff let out a sigh of relief when lunch came to the table. He really thought he stuck his foot in his mouth and could feel Jocelyn backing away. He really liked her and didn't think there was a protocol he should follow. He thought putting it all on the table, letting her know what he wanted, was a good thing. He was starting to re-think that.

He could also tell there was something else on Jocelyn's mind. He didn't know if it was work related or personal, but she definitely wasn't the receptive person she was the night before. Jeff wanted to ask if there was something wrong, but hesitated because he didn't want to seem pushy.

They ate lunch in virtual silence. Jocelyn's mind wandered back to wondering who gave Terrell her phone number. So much for not worrying about it and not persecuting anyone for it, she thought. She was also thinking Jeff put a lot of pressure on her. What he was saying was that he knew what he wanted so she must match it, or it won't work.

"A penny for your thoughts?" asked Jeff, interrupting the silence.

"No thoughts, just thinking through some things. What about you? You have been awfully silent," Jocelyn answered.

She hoped that would take the heat off her.

"I was just thinking about you and how you feel about what I told you," Jeff responded. "I hope I didn't scare you off."

"No, you haven't. I like a man who knows what he wants. Less confusion," Jocelyn answered with a grin.

That was a direct contrast from any of the men in her past. She had to take a survey just to see if they were in a relationship or not.

Jeff smiled, mostly in relief. He was happy he didn't scare her away, but she still wasn't completely with him. He wondered where she was and what she was really thinking about. Her face wasn't giving off signals of disinterest or anything that he could read. He really didn't think he was her problem.

When they completed lunch Jeff walked Jocelyn back to her office. She thanked him and kissed him on the cheek. He reached for her and turned her toward him. He tried to read her eyes one more time. He still wasn't certain what was bothering her, but he knew something was. He kissed her on the lips, and she responded. Jeff told Jocelyn to call him that night when she got settled in at home. Jocelyn nodded and went into her office building.

As soon as Jocelyn sat at her desk, she dialed her mother's phone number. She was doing a process of elimination of who could have given Terrell her phone number and her mother was the only one she could think of who would do that.

"Hi, Mom. How are you?" Jocelyn decided to make small talk before she dug in and asked her mother.

"I'm fine, how are you? Did you eat lunch?" Jocelyn's mother asked.

"Yeah, I ate lunch. Did you? Do you need me to pick you up anything on my way home from work?" Jocelyn answered her mother's inquiry.

"No. I'm fine. Is everything OK? I'm surprised you are calling in the middle of the day," her mother responded.

"Did you give Terrell my phone number?" Jocelyn couldn't hold it in any longer.

"Yes. He said he had something important to tell you," her mother answered.

"Mom! There was nothing important he had to tell me. He called three times last night while I was out on my date," Jocelyn said before she thought about what she was saying. She forgot she wasn't going to tell anyone about Jeff yet.

"Date? That's good. I'm sorry baby. I thought he was going to tell you he was finally going to do right by Lawanna and his son and marry that girl," Jocelyn's mother responded nonchalantly.

"Lawanna? That is the mother of his son. He told me he had a son yesterday in the mall but didn't mention it was with one of my friends from high school," Jocelyn answered.

"You saw him yesterday?" her mother asked.

"Yes, Mom, I saw him yesterday. If I wanted him to have my number, I would have given it to him. That's why I always tell you to ask me before you give anyone my number," Jocelyn answered, annoyed.

Jocelyn wasn't annoyed at her mother. She was annoyed at Terrell and the nerve he had to mess with one of her friends.

"Well, I'm sorry. I had no idea. You don't have to take that tone with me," Her mother answered.

Jocelyn thought about it. She didn't mean to upset her mother. "I'm sorry, Mom. I am not mad at you. I just wish you had asked me first. OK?" Jocelyn told her to calm her down. "I love you. I will call you tonight. I have to go."

Jocelyn hung up and called Monique. She really couldn't believe what she was hearing. She wanted to know if Monique already knew.

"Hey Monique. Who is Lawanna's baby father?" Jocelyn asked after they greeted each other on the phone.

"When did Lawanna have a baby?" Monique asked. "Is Michael

her baby's daddy?"

"No, not Michael. Terrell is her baby's daddy," Jocelyn informed Monique.

"Get out of here. Who told you that?" Monique asked. She was laughing.

"My mother told me. She knew all along," Jocelyn told Monique.

"Get out. She never told you? Why? I thought she would have loved to show you Terrell was no good," Monique said. She was in shock, but she also wanted to know more.

"I don't know why she hadn't told me before. She told me she gave him my number because she thought he wanted to tell me he was going to do right by Lawanna and their son," Jocelyn said in a mocking voice. "Maybe that was her way of reminding me he is no good. She didn't have to drop the bomb then."

"Yep. Slip it in so you don't know why she is telling you that. Too funny," Monique said. "I thought you were telling me that trifling Michael was hitting off more of my friends."

Monique was laughing now but she was devastated when Michael was doing it.

"What are you going to say to Terrell?" Monique ended the silence.

"Nothing. He is none of my business. Good luck to them," Jocelyn answered.

"Good luck to them? You know he ain't going to marry that girl. He was just trying to chase you down yesterday," Monique answered Jocelyn back.

Jocelyn told Monique he could save all of that and she definitely didn't have anything to say to him. Monique said OK and told Jocelyn she had to get back to work. Jocelyn said bye and said she should do the same, but she knew her day was shot to hell. She couldn't believe this, any of it.

There was a voicemail from Jeff on Jocelyn's phone when she got home. She wasn't in the mood to talk or go out, so she decided not to return the call. She put the phone on the charger before she went upstairs to take a bath. She figured a bath would take some of the stress of the past few days off. She was running the water when the phone rang again.

She ran down thinking it was Jeff. She was disappointed when she saw it was Terrell. She knew not even a bath would help her wash him away. She walked away from the phone. That was until she saw that he had left a message.

"Hey sweetheart. I figured you would be home from work by now. I guess you must be out with your boyfriend or something," Terrell said it like he knew she was home.

Jocelyn called him back, "How dare you call me?"

"What? What's wrong?" Terrell said.

He sounded shocked and a little wounded.

"You! Tell me what's wrong Terrell. Tell me who your baby's mama is?" Jocelyn answered him.

"Oh. Why do you care about that? That has nothing to do with us," he said nonchalantly.

"Are you kidding me? You screw one of my friends and get her pregnant, and you think that has nothing to do with us?" Jocelyn was yelling. She knew she was yelling but she couldn't stop.

She thought about it. She shouldn't have answered the phone. She continued. "You know what. It doesn't have anything to do with us because there is no us. Damn, I'm glad about that."

"Are you? If you are so happy, why are you angry about Lawanna?" Terrell asked.

"Are you kidding me? I know you lack good judgment and morals but to ask me why I am upset about you being with one of my friends is ridiculous. How would you feel if I talked to one of your boys and got pregnant by him? Lord knows enough of your so-called friends have tried to talk to me. There are just some things you don't do."

"Who made up this code Jocelyn?" Terrell asked. "Furthermore, Lawanna told me you weren't really friends."

Jocelyn just laughed at Terrell. She thought his nerve was unbelievable. Who made that code up, she thought.

"So, how would you feel?" Jocelyn asked.

"What?" Terrell asked. "How would I feel, what?"

"If I got with one of your friends?" Jocelyn asked Terrell. She couldn't understand why she was even indulging him.

"You wouldn't do that," Terrell answered.

Jocelyn laughed out loud. "How do you know I haven't?"

"Have you?" Terrell asked. "Stop playing with me. Someone would have told me."

"Really? Figure out which one. It happened." Jocelyn was still laughing. Terrell was beginning to believe her, and he didn't like this conversation.

"I don't have a problem with it. I don't care which one it was. I think he is foul though," Terrell answered. "He should have known better."

"Terrell, who made up that code? We weren't together so it doesn't matter." Jocelyn gave him his own line and he didn't like it at all.

"Shit, you should have known better. It's different from what happened with Lawanna. I didn't know she knew you when we got together," Terrell told Jocelyn.

"How does it feel, Terrell?" Jocelyn was just messing with him now. "Do you want to know who it was?"

"Naw, because I would kill that fool," Terrell said.

"Why?" Jocelyn asked. "It's all good right? Friends, cousins, brothers, etc., right?"

"You're taking it too far now. It better not have been a family member of mine," Terrell told Jocelyn. "Now you're talking reckless."

"What are you going to do? Not a damn thing," Jocelyn told him before she slammed down the phone. Damn, she hated cell phones. It didn't have the emphasis it did back in the day.

Terrell tried to call Jocelyn back two times, but she didn't answer. She went back to the bathroom and ran the water for her bath again. She couldn't understand why she let Terrell get to her. She looked around for her Lavender scented candles and bath oil. It is supposed to calm you down, she thought, please, let it work tonight.

She rewound the conversation with Terrell back in her head. It was possible Terrell didn't know she and Lawanna were friends in high school, but it didn't matter. He stayed with her after he found out. She couldn't believe he had the audacity to say she wouldn't get with any of his friends, but he didn't see anything wrong with being with one of hers. Damn, this Lavender wasn't working.

Jocelyn cleared her mind and closed her eyes. She was trying to relax but couldn't. She just lay there in the bubbles, trying not to think or move. She began to relax. She did some of the meditation exercises she learned in Yoga class. She thought to herself that she needed to start going back to the gym, especially that class.

Jocelyn got out of her bath and wrapped a robe around her body. She didn't dry off and giggled at the squishy noise she made as she walked around. She picked up the phone and called Jeff. He wasn't at home, so she checked her phone to see where the call came from. His work number was where the last call came from so, she called there.

"Hey." Jeff answered on the second ring.

"Hey? What are you still doing at work?" Jocelyn asked Jeff.

"It's only 8:30. I've been here a lot later than this," Jeff told Jocelyn.

"When are you going to leave work?" Jocelyn asked.

"Why? You feel like going out?" Jeff asked. "I can wrap it up and meet you."

"No, I don't feel like going out. I feel like staying in," Jocelyn answered. "I just took a bath with this Lavender bath oil; I think you should try it. It relaxes you."

"Relax. What's that?" Jeff asked. "I need to try that. Do I get company with the bath oil?"

"Well, I already took a bath, but I'll see what I can do," Jocelyn told Jeff with a laugh. "Maybe I can find someone to rub your back."

"I'll be right there. Give me about a half an hour," Jeff answered quickly. He answered like he thought Jocelyn was going to change her mind.

Chapter 7

Jeff got to Jocelyn's house in a little less than an hour. He apologized and told her his boss had called to check on a file. He looked at Jocelyn and saw she had a robe on, and wondered if she had anything under the robe. He also noticed she had another robe in her hand and wondered if it was for him.

"Off with your shoes sir," Jocelyn told Jeff.

Jeff obeyed.

"Now the coat," Jocelyn told Jeff. Jeff obliged and then started to take his suit jacket off also.

"Why are you taking that off?" Jocelyn asked. "I didn't tell you to take that off." She was messing with him now.

Jeff stopped mid-action and looked at Jocelyn.

Jocelyn laughed at Jeff and told him he could take the jacket off. She gave him the robe and told him she would go run his bath water while he changed. He motioned for her to come close to him. When she did, he kissed her. She smiled and began to walk off. He pulled her back and kissed her again. He repeated this until she told him the bath water was not going to run itself.

Jeff began taking off his clothes and realized he shouldn't have kissed her like that. He hoped Jocelyn didn't notice him bulging through the robe. He put the robe on and examined himself in the hall mirror. It wasn't as evident as he thought so he headed upstairs.

When Jeff got to the top of the stairs he called out to Jocelyn. He didn't know which room she was in. He followed her voice through her bedroom until he was standing in the bathroom. He was amazed at the size of her tub.

"You can fit a couple of people in there," Jeff said. He thought it might sound like an invitation, so he continued. "It's a nice size tub."

"Get in," Jocelyn told Jeff. "I'll cover my eyes while you disrobe."

Jocelyn turned and faced the wall. Jeff laughed and obeyed.

"You didn't have to cover your eyes. We are both adults," Jeff told her.

"Are you trying to get fresh with me?" Jocelyn asked.

"No, not at all. I was just saying," Jeff answered. "I am just going to sit here and be quiet. Thank you."

Jeff thought about how he was feeling and thought it was good. Jocelyn turned around. He didn't want her to think all he wanted is sex. She was right about the bath though. It was very relaxing. He could still feel himself growing under the water. He didn't know what to do about it. If he touched it, it would only get worse.

Jocelyn was in the bedroom looking for a CD to put in the CD player. She found one Monique made her. It had a lot of slow songs on it. She popped it in and went back to the bathroom.

"Doesn't that feel good?" Jocelyn asked Jeff.

Jeff panicked and put his hands over his penis, begging it to go down.

"What's wrong?" Jocelyn asked.

"Nothing. You startled me. I'm fine," Jeff answered.

"So how was your day counselor?" Jocelyn asked as she sat on the edge of the tub.

Jeff started talking about what he did after he left her. Yeah, that worked. Just the thought of work made the stiffness go away. He looked up at Jocelyn. He thought to himself she was still not acting like the person he met a few weeks ago. He grabbed her hand and asked her how her afternoon was. She smiled and asked if he wanted her to rub his back.

Jeff moved up in the tub and Jocelyn got in behind him. She rubbed his shoulders and Jeff began to moan. He was so tense, and the massage was definitely hitting the spot. Jocelyn laughed at Jeff and told him he had to find ways to channel his stress. She told him she could feel knots in his shoulders and back. She continued to massage Jeff and he began to relax.

Jeff was almost to the point of falling asleep when Jocelyn splashed him with water. He turned and faced her, asking her what that was for. He glanced at Jocelyn, and she didn't move or cover herself. He slid up and kissed her. She still didn't move, so he kissed her again. This time it was longer, and he could feel himself getting hard again.

Jocelyn moved then. She could feel him up against her stomach, so she pushed him back. Jocelyn wasn't sure she wanted to take it there with Jeff. Actually, she was sure she didn't. He moved back to the other side of the tub and apologized to Jocelyn. He laughed it off and said he guessed he relaxed a little too much.

"It's OK. I'm just not ready to go there. We're still getting to know each other," Jocelyn told Jeff. She thought about the past and how didn't want to rush into sex with him –she wanted to keep him.

"No problem, that's not why I came here. I'm in no rush," Jeff told Jocelyn. "I think we should get out of this tub though."

"You get out and then I'll get out," Jocelyn told Jeff, hoping he'd understand.

Jeff began to get out of the tub. He thought it was amazing but good. He thought to himself, he really got a good girl. He smiled to himself because that never happens to him.

He put the robe on and went out of the bathroom. Jocelyn got out of the tub, a little disappointed with herself. She thought she would get with Jeff to get Terrell out of her mind. She felt sad she couldn't go through with it. She put on her robe and went out to her bedroom. Jeff was gone. She thought he must have left the house.

She went downstairs and he was sitting on the couch. He had put his pants and shirt back on.

"Are you leaving?" Jocelyn asked Jeff.

"Do you want me to leave?" Jeff asked.

"You don't have to. You didn't have to put all those clothes on either." Jocelyn grinned at Jeff.

"Oh, I thought it would be best. I am OK. This is my second skin." Jeff told her.

Jeff motioned for Jocelyn to come sit next to him on the couch. She did and he came close. He kissed her on the cheek.

"I'm not mad at you," Jeff told Jocelyn. "Actually, I am kind of happy we didn't take it there."

"Really?" Jocelyn asked him.

"Yeah, we have plenty of time for that," Jeff said, looking pointedly at his lap. "I don't listen to him anyway. He would get me in all kinds of trouble."

Jeff began laughing to ease the mood. Jocelyn laughed with him. He pulled Jocelyn close and laid her on top of him on the couch.

"What's bothering you?" Jeff asked her. "Don't tell me nothing because I see it in your eyes."

"It's really nothing. Something silly I guess," Jocelyn told him. She continued. "My ex-boyfriend had a child with one of my friends from high school. I don't know why it is bothering me."

"Did he do it on purpose? Did he know she was your friend?" Jeff asked. "Because if he did that is wrong."

Jocelyn looked at Jeff. She couldn't believe he understood. "He said he didn't know until after," Jocelyn told Jeff.

Jocelyn smiled at Jeff. She is thinking of a way to change the subject.

"How rude of me. I haven't offered you anything to eat or drink. Have you eaten dinner yet?" Jocelyn asked.

"You know what? I haven't eaten. I was going to pick something up on my way home from work," Jeff said. He had not thought about eating at all since Jocelyn called him. "Let's go out and get something," Jeff continued. He was starting to feel hungry now that the subject of food had been brought up.

"OK, but I have food in the house," Jocelyn told Jeff. "I can easily whip you up some noodles."

They both laughed and Jeff answered, "Although that sounds tempting, I think it will be good for us to go out."

Jocelyn wondered why he thought so but didn't ask. She wondered if he was upset about what didn't happen upstairs.

"Are you upset with me?" Jocelyn asked Jeff.

Jeff gave Jocelyn a shocked look and said, "No! Not at all. We have plenty of time to get to that point. I have no problem with waiting." He was being honest.

"OK, because I don't want you to think I am playing games with you. I am not. I didn't mean to lead you here under the pretense we were going to have sex," Jocelyn said hesitantly. She looked him right in his eyes to see if she could gauge his response.

"I don't feel like you misled me, and I did enjoy the bath. It was relaxing. Like I said, I relaxed a little too much and felt comfortable with you," Jeff told Jocelyn. He continued by telling her, "I like you. I've let you know every step of the way. I didn't mean to offend you and I don't think any less of you because we didn't have sex. If anything, I think more of you."

Jocelyn was shocked by Jeff's response, but she could tell by the look in his eyes that he was being sincere. She really liked him too. She thought about it and realized if it was any of the other man she has dated, she would have probably had to throw them out of her house. Jeff's attitude was very refreshing.

"There you go thinking again." Jeff broke Jocelyn's train of thought.

"How could you tell?" Jocelyn asked.

"Well, this time there is a frown line on your forehead," Jeff said laughing. "Are you still thinking about your ex?"

"No, I was thinking about you," Jocelyn said and could see the confusion in Jeff's eyes. She continued, "Not exactly you, but this situation and how you are handling it. I was thinking I would have had to throw most men out by now. You are being a complete gentleman and I am really impressed."

"That made your frown line pop up?" Jeff asked with a laugh.

"No, thinking about all the fools in my past I would have had to throw out made the frown line appear," Jocelyn answered and laughed with him.

"Not me. I'm no gentleman though. That's part of the reason I want to go out to dinner. I want you to feel comfortable with me," Jeff answered.

"Ohh, I thought it was the thought of eating my cooking that made you suggest going out." Jocelyn laughed again. She was relieved at his honesty. "I will go upstairs and get dressed."

"OK. I'll be here. Is there a bathroom down here?" Jeff asked.

Jeff really needed to wash his face with cold water. He was really feeling the effects of being so close to Jocelyn, knowing there was nothing between them but her robe. He felt so embarrassed about having no control tonight. He thought to himself it had been a while since he had been around a woman, especially one he liked so much, and chalked it up to that. It made him feel a little better about reacting like a twelve-year-old boy with a crush on his teacher.

Jeff didn't hear Jocelyn when she told him there was a bathroom in the hallway leading to the kitchen. He asked her again and she answered him again from upstairs. He got in the bathroom and splashed his face with water. He looked himself over to make sure there was no leftover bulge from earlier. He tucked his shirt in and put his tie back on before returning to sit on the couch.

Jocelyn came downstairs about ten minutes later. She had on a pair of fitted cotton pants and a silk button shirt. They were both a deep purple color which brought out her eyes.

"I didn't know where we were going so, I hope this will do," Jocelyn said when she reached the bottom of the stairs.

Jeff looked at her and told her, "That will definitely do." Jeff was thinking in his mind that maybe he should have called it a night earlier. He started feeling tingly again. "You look incredible," he said, nodding his head in approval.

He rushed Jocelyn out of the house. He decided it was best to leave before she had to throw him out. He wanted to touch her, kiss her, something, but thought it was too risky. He just opened the car door for her and then went around to his side to get in. He got in the car and thought it would be safer to kiss her in there. So, he did. Jocelyn let out a giggle and it startled Jeff.

"What's so funny?" Jeff asked. He was looking around, but he didn't want to look down.

"Nothing is funny. You startled me," Jocelyn said to Jeff's relief.

"Oh sorry," Jeff told her.

"No problem. I can't think of a better way to be startled." Jocelyn told him.

Jeff asked Jocelyn what she felt like eating. Jocelyn had no idea. They sat in the car for a moment and decided on Thai food. They drove to Newbury Street to one of their favorite restaurants, but there were no tables and the waiting list was an hour long—at least that is what the maître d' told them.

When they got back to the car, Jocelyn asked Jeff if he would be too disappointed if they called it a night. It was already ten thirty at night and they probably wouldn't find anything to eat this late anyway. Jeff looked at Jocelyn and told her he wasn't disappointed, and he would take her home. When they reached her house Jeff got out and opened the door for Jocelyn.

He walked her to the front door and gave her a kiss on the forehead. To his surprise, she reached up and kissed him on the lips when he let her head go. She pulled him close to her and thanked him for tonight. He nodded and told her he would call her tomorrow from work and possibly they could make plans for the weekend. She nodded, they kissed one more time and he walked away.

Chapter 8

Jocelyn's mom called her at work. This scared Jocelyn because her mom never called her there.

"Mama what's wrong?" Jocelyn asked.

"Nothing, baby. Your father and I are having a cookout on Saturday. We just decided this morning. I am making sure everyone knows. Feel free to bring a date," her mother told her.

"Ah ha that's what this is about. That's why I didn't want to tell anyone about Jeff yet. I will see if he wants to come to your cookout," Jocelyn told her mother and laughed at how obvious this whole thing was.

"Oh, what is he too good for 'our' cookout?" Jocelyn's mother asked her after catching her tone. "If he is, you can leave him in his bourgeois world."

Jocelyn was shaking her head. She didn't know what else to say to her but that she had to go, and she would ask Jeff if he would have the time to come to the cookout on Saturday. Jocelyn didn't understand how her mother got that Jeff was bourgeois from that conversation but anyway. Her mother told her OK and said she would see them on Saturday. Jocelyn wondered if her mother even heard her say Jeff may not have the time, but she just shook it off and tried to get some work done.

Jocelyn called Jeff around eleven. She hoped he wasn't at his desk so she could leave the invitation on his voicemail. Jeff picked up.

"Hey baby. How are you?" Jeff asked.

Jocelyn was about to ask how he knew it was her calling but remembered technology is a great thing.

"I'm fine, how are you?" Jocelyn answered. "Did you get any sleep last night?"

"I slept like a baby. After I dropped you off. I went to Wendy's, picked up a burger and headed home," Jeff answered.

Jocelyn had no idea why she asked him that question. She was trying to stall, but that question was out of left field.

"What can I do for the pretty lady? Are you in legal trouble or something?" Jeff asked.

He was amused by his joke, but it went right over Jocelyn's head.

"Huh?" Jocelyn asked. "Legal Trouble?"

She thought about it and after a second or so she got it. "Oh, no silly, not yet. My mother is having a cookout on Saturday, and she told me to invite you. Are you busy?"

"Absolutely not. I mean I have some work I am bringing home, but I can do it later tonight or Sunday," Jeff answered gleefully.

"Are you sure? My family is going to be there and although I slipped up and mentioned you to my mother, I am thinking it is too soon to meet the family," Jocelyn exclaimed hesitantly.

"No, not at all. I don't mind and I have been dying for a cookout. Please don't take the cookout from me now that you mentioned it to me."

Jeff was almost pleading. "I haven't been to a cookout since I went home last year. I'll be good."

Jocelyn couldn't help laughing. "I should have known you were excited about the food and not about meeting my family."

"Oh no. I will be glad to meet them too. I'm sorry if I sounded greedy," Jeff answered.

"I was only joking with you. You may not still feel that way after meeting them." He really was more excited about the food than what she told him. She was still laughing about his enthusiasm.

"What should I bring?" Jeff asked.

"Just you and your appetite. Mom usually makes too much food, and the neighbors have to come over to get plates because there is nowhere to put the leftovers." Jocelyn told Jeff she would see him Saturday.

"I have to wait until Saturday to see you?" Jeff asked.

"It's Friday, Saturday is not that long away," Jocelyn answered. "No really, did you have something planned?" she asked Jeff.

"No, nothing planned...just hopes. It's OK I can wait until tomorrow or call you tonight," said Jeff.

He didn't sound very happy about it.

"I was joking with you. If you want to get together, we can," Jocelyn told him.

She had noticed the change in his tone and didn't want him to think she didn't want to go out with him.

"Naw. It's cool. I can get some of the work done tonight and have more time to spend with you tomorrow," Jeff told her.

Jeff then told Jocelyn he had an appointment and will definitely give her a call later. She said OK and good-bye.

Jocelyn was up at seven thirty the next morning, pacing the floor. Jeff didn't call her like he said he would, and she didn't know if he was going to show up today. She was wondering why he hadn't called and was thinking about what she could tell her family if he didn't show up. At about eight o'clock she decided she was going to try to get more sleep and she wasn't going to worry about whether Jeff was coming with her today.

The phone rang. She rushed to pick it up, thinking it was Jeff, but it was Monique.

"Damn girl, why do you sound out of breath?" Monique asked when Jocelyn answered the phone.

"The phone woke me up out of a deep sleep. I am fine. What do you want?" Jocelyn asked Monique.

"Damn! What do I want? I was just calling to make sure you are coming over to your mother's house today. At least someone had the decency to invite me to the cookout," Monique told Jocelyn.

"I knew there was someone I forgot to call. Sorry girl. I'm not getting an attitude with you. You know how I am when I first wake up," Jocelyn told Monique. "I wonder who else my mother invited."

"You mean Terrell?" Monique asked. "I thought you had a new man."

"See, that's what I am talking about," Jocelyn said. "She is inviting everyone over to see my new man and you know she is trifling enough to invite Terrell, just so she can make sure he knows I have someone else."

Monique laughed at that. She knew that Jocelyn's mom would do it too.

"Worst part about it is I haven't heard from Jeff since I asked him to come yesterday morning," Jocelyn said hesitantly.

"His name is Jeff? Where is he from? I might know him," Monique told Jocelyn.

"I doubt it, girl. He is from New Jersey. He only came here to take a job about four months ago," Jocelyn told Monique. Jocelyn was rolling her eyes and thinking she knew where the conversation was headed, but she was glad Jeff was not from Boston.

"Good for you girl. You got an import because these men in Boston are no good," Monique said. "I was wondering who you could possibly be dating in this city I didn't know or know about. The city is so small."

Jocelyn laughed at Monique's response. Monique thought she knew everyone. That was probably why she was still single. She tried to make a connection between everyone and someone she may know. She had also begun adding more and more restrictions on who she would date when she'd broken up with Michael. Jocelyn had restrictions too, but some of Monique's were just ridiculous.

Jocelyn's other line beeped. She was a little happy because she wasn't in the mood for one of Monique's sermons about men being no good. She alerted Monique to the fact that the other line was beeping and told her it was probably her mom trying to find out if Jeff was coming. She told Monique, "You know my mom probably has a million questions. I will see you later because you know I won't be able to get her off the phone."

Monique said OK and they agreed to meet up later at the cookout before hanging up.

It wasn't Jocelyn's mother on the other end. It was Jeff.

"Hey lady, are we still on for today?" Jeff asked.

"I don't know, are we? I didn't hear from you last night. I thought you changed your mind," Jocelyn told Jeff.

"I'm sorry. I told you I had to bring some work home. I had to make a couple of phone calls and then go to the law library. By the time I got back it was after midnight and I didn't think it would be good to call that late," Jeff told her.

"OK. So here is the plan. You can drive here, and I will drive to the cookout in my car. It'll be easier that way," Jocelyn told Jeff. "Unless you feel you would need your car for something."

"I should be fine. My, are we formal? Are you sure everything is OK?" Jeff inquired.

"I'm fine. I'm sorry. I had it in my mind and said it while I remembered," Jocelyn responded. "What time do you want to get here?"

"What time did you have in mind? I told you I am all yours today," Jeff said.

This made Jocelyn smile. She liked the sound of it. "All mine? Hmmm," Jocelyn said laughing.

Jocelyn suggested Jeff get to her house at about two-thirty. Jeff told her he could do that and that he would see her then before they hung up. Jocelyn smiled as she reviewed Jeff's words one more time. "All hers!" She was snapped out of the thought by the telephone. She thought to herself, this must be Mom.

It wasn't her mother. It was Terrell.

"Hello J. How are you?" Terrell asked after Jocelyn said hello.

"I'm fine. What do you want, Terrell?" Jocelyn shot back.

"Your mom invited me to the cookout, and I wanted to know if it is OK with you," Terrell told her. "I also have my son. It's my weekend to have him and I wondered if it would be cool to bring him."

"It's fine by me Terrell. I don't know why you are asking me. It's my mother's cookout and if she doesn't have a problem with it, who am I to say no," Jocelyn said in a frustrated tone.

"OK. I just didn't want you to feel uncomfortable with me there or because I have my son. I am a considerate person. If you would have said you didn't want me or him there I wouldn't come." Terrell explained to Jocelyn. "Do you need a ride J? I can come pick you up."

"No, I don't need a ride. My friend and I are going to drive over," Jocelyn answered.

"Oh OK. Yeah. You and your friend will be driving over. I guess I'll see you there then," Terrell said.

Jocelyn could hear the disappointment in Terrell's voice.

"I look forward to meeting your son," Jocelyn said, trying to change the subject.

"Yeah. He's a great kid, very friendly. You should meet him," Terrell answered. She could hear the change in his voice.

"What's his name?" Jocelyn asked.

"He's a junior. She named him Terrell before I even knew he existed," Terrell answered.

"Before you knew he existed? What does that mean?" Jocelyn asked.

"I told you there was no big relationship. It was just a couple of nights, just enough for a slipup." Terrell let out a little grin with the last statement.

"But nobody told you she was pregnant?" Jocelyn asked.

"Nope. No one told me a thing. I saw her once during her pregnancy and she never mentioned she was pregnant or that it was mine. He was three months old before I knew about him," Terrell told Jocelyn. He continued by saying, "I probably wouldn't have found out then if she was able to get an apartment and assistance. But you know they passed those laws saying you have to have a father's name on the birth certificate to get anything."

"Yeah, I know that. Are you sure he's yours?" Jocelyn asked before she knew what she was saying.

"Yeah, we went through all of that before I paid her a cent. I purposely didn't pay her so I could go to court and request a paternity test. He's mine. He looks a lot like me too. You'll see."

Jocelyn noticed Terrell perked up a little when he said that. She was wondering why but chalked it up to him being proud about his son.

"Well, I have to go, Terrell. My friend will be here soon, and I haven't even showered. I will see you at the cookout," Jocelyn told Terrell.

Jocelyn didn't know what to think about Terrell's admissions. She wondered why Lawanna didn't want Terrell to know he was the father. She was probably going to use it against him later on. Jocelyn thought hard but couldn't think of any other reason. She thought about the fact Lawanna named the little boy after him but didn't tell him about him. All of it seemed very weird but it was none of her business. Terrell was someone else's problem now.

Chapter 9

Jocelyn and Jeff arrived at the cookout at about three thirty that afternoon. Jocelyn stalled by acting like she was looking for a parking space. After searching for a while, she gave up and drove right up to the garage and pulled in. She could see Jeff give her a weird look out of the corner of her eye.

"Baby? Why did you try to park on the street if you could park in the garage?" Jeff asked. "Are you nervous? Do you want to be here?"

"Yeah, I'm fine. I just thought someone would probably park in front of the garage or in the driveway," Jocelyn answered. "After I didn't find a spot. I just took a shot. I wasn't thinking. I guess I could make the person move their car."

"OK. It's going to be fine. I promise not to embarrass you," Jeff said with a smile.

"I'm not worried about that. I'm worried about them embarrassing me. That's why I trapped you here. You couldn't go running in the hills." Jocelyn laughed back at Jeff. "Naw, you see how the parking is. You have New Jersey plates and no neighborhood sticker. They would probably tow your car."

They walked in and Monique ran right up and hugged Jocelyn, all the time looking over Jocelyn's shoulder at Jeff. When Jocelyn pulled away, she noticed Monique looked a little disappointed. She tried to hide it with a smile, but Jocelyn knew her. Jocelyn introduced them and told Monique she would catch up with her later.

Jocelyn made her way into the house to the kitchen. That is where she knew she would find her mother. Sure enough her mother was there delegating tasks and still cooking. Jocelyn didn't even want to know how much food was already outside. She knew there was food out there because some people were already eating.

"Mom. Mom!" Jocelyn yelled out to her mother.

Jocelyn's mother turned around when she finished barking out directions and answered Jocelyn.

Jocelyn's mother came over and hugged Jocelyn. Her mother did the same thing Monique did. Jocelyn's mother whispered, "He's handsome," in Jocelyn's ear.

Jocelyn laughed and broke away from her mother. "Mom, this is Jeff and Jeff this is my mom." Jocelyn introduced them. She was holding Jeff by the hand.

"Hello Mrs..." Jeff stopped. At that moment he realized he didn't know Jocelyn's last name.

"McCrary," Jocelyn's mother completed it for him. "But you can call me Sis, everyone but Jocelyn does." She was laughing but Jeff was truly embarrassed. How could he have never asked Jocelyn her last name?

Jocelyn grabbed Jeff by the hand and asked where she could find her father. Her mother said he is in the living room, watching some game. Jocelyn looked up at Jeff and asked if he watched sports. She noticed the troubled look on his face and asked him what was wrong.

"How could I not know your last name?" Jeff asked. "I didn't even ask."

"It's fine." Jocelyn told him.

"Do you know my last name?" Jeff asked.

"It's Johnson. I only know that because you gave me your business card. You put my numbers in your cell phone," Jocelyn told him. She was trying to reason with him, but he was still distraught.

"You better get that look off your face. My dad is like a shark. He'll sense your fear," joked Jocelyn.

Jeff gave her a semi-smile and apologized. She reached up and kissed him on the forehead. He looked down and kissed her on the mouth. When they opened their eyes Jocelyn's father was right in their faces. Jeff extended his hand, but Jocelyn's father just looked at him.

"Dad, you can stop trying to act hard. I already told him you are a pushover," Jocelyn said and nudged her father in the belly.

"Aww! Everyone is always ruining my fun. I could have scared him, you know," Mr. McCrary said with a chuckle. He reached out and shook Jeff's hand. "How are you doing son? Pay me no mind. No one else around here does."

"I'm fine. How are you sir?" Jeff answered.

"Call me Joe, son," Mr. McCrary told Jeff. "You're going to help out on the grill, right?"

"I can do that," Jeff said. His eyes lit up. Jocelyn wondered why. She looked at her father and he took her cue.

"Well, see you out there, son," Mr. McCrary told Jeff and walked off.

"What are you so happy about?" Jocelyn asked after her father left.

"They are nice, and I love grilling. I'd have one at my apartment if they would let me. I always do the grilling at home," Jeff answered.

Jocelyn shook her head. She told Jeff he was too much and warned him her father would disappear and leave him on the grill for the rest of the day. She kissed Jeff one more time. When she began to walk away, he pulled her back and kissed her again.

"Come on, let's get you something to eat before it is time for your grill duty," Jocelyn told Jeff.

"OK." Jeff answered cheerfully. He wrapped his arms around Jocelyn and followed her back to the backyard. When they reached the back door Jocelyn saw Terrell coming in through the gate.

"Who is that baby? Your brother?" Jeff asked.

Jeff noticed he parked in the driveway.

"No. Why would you ask that?" Jocelyn was curious why Jeff would think that.

"I know you have a brother and I see he parked in the driveway," Jeff answered.

Jeff was even more curious to know who he was now.

"He did it out of habit. That is my ex-boyfriend," Jocelyn answered before she thought about what she was saying.

She looked back to catch the expression on Jeff's face but didn't see one.

"Oh, OK," Jeff answered. "I take it that is the little man you were upset about the other day."

"Yes, but I am over that now and I am over him. He is still close to the family, though, because we dated for a long time," Jocelyn told Jeff.

Jocelyn thought of a way to make Jeff feel secure.

"OK. I understand," Jeff answered. Jocelyn wondered if he really did.

Terrell came right up to them. He extended his hand to Jeff and gave Jocelyn a kiss on the cheek.

"This is little T, my son," Terrell said, proudly holding him by the head. "Say hi, T."

Jocelyn bent down to Jr.'s level and said hi. He looked up at

Terrell and then he looked back at Jocelyn. He finally said hi and then Jocelyn asked if he wanted juice or something to drink. He nodded his head yes, so Jocelyn took him by the hand into the kitchen. As soon as they got in the kitchen, her mom gave her a strange look.

"You traded the tall, handsome one in for a little cute one?" she asked Jocelyn.

"No, this is Terrell's son," Jocelyn answered.

Jocelyn's mother shot her a concerned look.

"What ma?" Jocelyn responded to her mother's look.

"I didn't say anything. What do you need?" She answered Jocelyn's question.

"He needs juice," Jocelyn answered. "I am only being polite because Terrell called me and said he wouldn't come if I didn't want him to. I told him I am OK with everything, and I am showing him that I am."

Jeff didn't stand around and talk to Terrell. He walked off right after Jocelyn. He went over to the grill and began talking to Joe.

"I'm just getting an idea of how you run your ship," Jeff started the conversation.

"It's over, son," Joe answered.

"Huh?" Jeff asked.

"Between Joce and Terrell. It's over and has been for a long time," Joe repeated.

"I'm not worried about that. I knew about him. She talked about him," Jeff said, masking his concern.

"OK. I just wanted to say it just in case you needed to hear it," Joe told Jeff and chuckled. "You ain't ready for the grill yet. Go mingle, son."

Jocelyn noticed Jeff was gone when she came back out. She asked Terrell what he said to Jeff. Terrell told Jocelyn he didn't say anything because Jeff walked off right after she did.

"Damn Joce, I wouldn't do that to you," Terrell answered her question.

"Sorry, Terrell," Jocelyn said.

She looked at Terrell for a minute because no one called her Joce anymore but her father.

"What could I have said to him? He knows about me, right?" Terrell asked.

"Yeah, he knows about you. He knows it's over. I don't have anything to hide," Jocelyn told Terrell before she let Jr.'s hand go and walked off.

Jocelyn walked over and looked at her father. He nodded at Jocelyn and blew her a kiss. She pretended she was snatching the kiss out of the air. They both chuckled loudly. Jeff watched that and began to smile too. He thought to himself he really had a good one and he wanted to keep her. He was smiling so broad that Jocelyn came and asked him why he was smiling.

"I'm loving this. All your family and friends are here. It's making me a little homesick, but I like this. Thanks for inviting me," Jeff told Jocelyn.

"You are welcome. When I slipped and told my mother I went on a date the other day, it was over. She would have kept hounding me until I brought you around," Jocelyn answered. She reached up and kissed Jeff again. Jeff seemed a little nervous.

"He's fine with it," Jocelyn told Jeff.

Jeff looked at Jocelyn and smiled before kissing her again.

Jeff's turn on the grill came up after Jocelyn's uncle. Her uncle's tour of duty was short because he started complaining about his back. Her father turned to Jocelyn and asked if they could borrow Jeff. She made them promise not to have him on the grill all night before she allowed him to go. Jocelyn asked Jeff if he needed her to keep him company. Jeff waved her off and then told her she could come if she wanted to.

Jocelyn watched for a while, and they talked about their childhoods. He told Jocelyn how impressed he was with her family and the closeness they shared. Jocelyn began to blush and played it off by asking if Jeff wanted something to drink. He told her that would be great, so she left to find him something.

As soon as Jocelyn went over to the cooler, Monique approached her.

"What, you're too good to hang with your girls because you have a man?" Monique asked.

Monique laughed it off and said she was only joking but Jocelyn could hear a hint of honesty in her tone.

Jocelyn answered, "I just don't want Jeff to feel uncomfortable, leaving him with a bunch of strangers. We'll come over after he finishes on the grill."

"I said I was only joking. Y'all are cute anyway. I still think I know him from somewhere or seen him with someone," Monique said.

She shook her head and left it at that.

"How is Terrell going to take seeing you with someone else?" Monique asked with a grin.

"Better than you are," Jocelyn said laughing. "No seriously, he hasn't said anything about it. He is probably so shook—I told him off about having a baby with Lawanna. He wasn't even going to come today, or so he said."

Monique laughed at that. She wanted to know more but Jocelyn pulled her hand out of the cooler and announced there were no more beers in there, so she was going into the house to get one for Jeff. She reminded Monique she would be back, and she was going to bring Jeff over to meet everyone. Monique said OK and went back over to the table she was sitting at, probably to spread the little bit of gossip she got out of Jocelyn.

Jocelyn walked into the kitchen, and it was surprisingly quiet. She couldn't believe someone actually got her mother out of the kitchen. She searched the refrigerator and then the freezer for a beer but to no avail. When she lifted her head out of the freezer and turned around Terrell was standing right in front of her.

"Hey, Joce. What are you looking for?" Terrell asked.

"A beer for Jeff. Do you know where they put them?" Jocelyn asked.

"Naw. Tell me about Jeff," Terrell inquired. "He seems like a cool brother."

Jocelyn looked at Terrell and he seemed to be sincere, so she started to tell him about Jeff. "He's great. He's a gentleman, kind, caring, and ambitious. He's pretty much everything I have ever wanted in a man."

"So, you love him more than you love me?" Terrell asked.

Jocelyn was shocked but she recovered and told Terrell, "I love him differently than I love you. You can't love two people the same because no two people are the same."

"So, you don't love me anymore?" Terrell asked and got right in Jocelyn's face. "Was I everything that you wanted in a man?"

Terrell got so close Jocelyn swore he was going to kiss her. She really didn't want to answer his questions and was getting bothered by him being that close to her.

"I guess you were everything I wanted when we met," Jocelyn answered one of his questions.

"So, you don't love me anymore?" Terrell asked and got even closer. This time he was breathing on her face, and it was making her nervous. He continued by whispering in her ear, "Remember the day I made love to you on this very counter? How worried you were that someone would walk in, and we wouldn't know it because the refrigerator was blocking the view?" Terrell laughed in Jocelyn's ear, but she was not laughing. Jocelyn went to push Terrell away and he grabbed her arms and brought her close to him.

"Why won't you answer my question, Joce? Do you still love me or not?" Terrell asked Jocelyn with almost a wicked grin. He was enjoying the fact that she seemed nervous about the question.

Jocelyn really didn't want to answer his question and was relieved when she heard Jeff's voice.

"Your dad told me there is no more beer and he sent someone to get some. I just wanted to let you know because I know you left to get me one," Jeff said, looking at Jocelyn and Terrell. "Well, I'm going back to the grill. Your dad only relieved me so I could find you and tell you that."

Jocelyn broke loose from Terrell and gave him a hard look. She ran after Jeff and joined him at the grill. She watched him, not knowing what he was thinking or what to say to him.

"Talk to me, Jeff," Jocelyn told Jeff.

"About what?" Jeff asked. "That was nothing right? I'm fine. I'm not an insecure man."

"Are you sure you are fine? It was really nothing. He was thanking me for letting him come today and for being nice to his son," Jocelyn said.

She was still looking at Jeff to gauge his response. There really wasn't one. She thought of how enraged Terrell would have been if he walked in on her, hugged up with another man and couldn't believe Jeff wasn't mad.

"OK. I believe you, Jocelyn. You have been honest with me, even about Terrell and your feelings about his son and him, so I have no reason not to believe you," Jeff answered. Jocelyn was so surprised and impressed by Jeff's reaction. She reached up to him and kissed him. Jeff didn't flinch this time. Jocelyn was happy because she thought it meant he was getting used to her family.

"Watch yourself. I don't want you to get burned by the grill," Jeff said as he pushed Jocelyn away.

Jeff then moved to the other side of the grill and worked from there. Jocelyn didn't know how to react to this and wasn't sure he wasn't being sincere about not wanting her to get burned. Jocelyn went to a chair right near the grill and sat down. She watched Jeff for a while before she spoke.

"You really take your grilling seriously?" Jocelyn asked, laughing.

"I told you that. I love to grill," Jeff answered her.

"I am enjoying the view, watching a handsome man, hard at work; there is something real sexy about that," Jocelyn told Jeff.

"Really?" Jeff inquired. "How sexy?"

"Very sexy," Jocelyn answered and blew Jeff a kiss.

Jeff thought about what he saw and decided it was not worth getting mad about. He dropped it and went over to Jocelyn and gave her a kiss.

"Mm mm. Thank you," Jocelyn said to Jeff. She felt in her mind everything was ok when he kissed her. "Can I have another?" Jocelyn joked.

Jeff obliged and reached down and kissed her again. In the distance they heard Jocelyn's father telling Jeff not to burn up all the food while making out with his daughter. They both laughed and Jeff eased back over to the grill. Jocelyn's father yelled thank you to Jeff and went back to playing cards. Jocelyn couldn't help but laugh at her father. She turned around to face him and he smiled at her.

A little while later Terrell came over to take over grilling duties. Jeff didn't want to leave but Jocelyn told Jeff she wanted to give him a tour of the house. Terrell looked a little disappointed because he knew what that was code for—she wanted to be alone with Jeff. Jeff caught on too and handed Terrell the fork.

Inside the house Jocelyn showed Jeff the living room, dining room, and then the rooms upstairs. Jeff inquired about Jocelyn's bedroom, and she told him they turned it into the guest bedroom. The only reason they didn't do the same to her brother's bedroom was because they weren't sure he wouldn't be back. He was in the Army and was away, so they weren't sure where he would stay when he came back.

She opened the door to what used to be her bedroom. She took him over to the closet to show him where all her childhood things were. When they stepped into the closet, she kissed Jeff. She grabbed him by the head and kissed him long and hard. She closed the closet door behind him and told him to be very quiet. She burst out laughing when he asked her if she had done this before.

"Very funny," Jocelyn answered.

"Ohhh!! You have had boys in your bedroom and closet?" Jeff asked. "How naughty."

"What are you going to do about it?" Jocelyn asked.

Jeff wasn't sure. He thought back to the other night when they got so close but then Jocelyn pulled away. He didn't know if he could go through that again. Jocelyn kissed him again and backed up. She pulled his shirt over his head and stared at him.

He looked at her and reached out to unbutton her shirt. He unbuttoned one button and looked at her. He did the same when he unbuttoned the second button. When he didn't get a response from Jocelyn he continued until all the buttons were unbuttoned. Then he slid her skirt down and watched it hit the floor.

He pulled Jocelyn close to him so she could feel that he was serious. He also did this to see if she was going to back away. She didn't. She began rubbing his chest and then she slid a hand down his stomach and into his pants. Jeff was shocked and excited. She fondled his dick and kissed him even harder than she did before.

She then removed her hand and grabbed Jeff by the head again. She backed them up to the wall. Jeff unfastened his belt and his pants and heard them hit the floor. He left his boxers on just in case Jocelyn stopped him, he still wasn't sure. He reached around Jocelyn and unhooked her bra. He pulled it off and stared at her breasts. He then took one and put it in his mouth. He bit it and she moaned.

Jeff then began to fondle her breast, moving his mouth from one to the other. He looked at her and she was definitely feeling it, so he pulled her panties down. He followed her panties down her legs and kissed her thighs until he reached the inside. He licked around her and then put one of her legs over his shoulder.

He played around in her with his tongue until Jocelyn started screaming and banging on the wall. He wanted to laugh but didn't want to break Jocelyn's mood. He picked her up and she wrapped her legs around his waist. He put his penis in, and she screamed again. He was worried about her screaming; not only because he thought someone would hear her, but he also wondered if it hurt her.

He got his answer to his second thought. She began sliding herself up and down on his penis, so he joined in. He was stroking and she was holding on to his neck so tight. He knew she was going to leave scratches, but he didn't care because it felt good. He turned around and let her gently down to the floor. He kissed her breast, biting them gently before he got on top of her.

He almost got the answer to his other thought. Jocelyn was screaming but he thought he heard someone calling her name. The person came into her bedroom and called her name again. It didn't sound like her mother, so Jeff wasn't that concerned. The person didn't immediately leave the room. It sounded like they were going through the things in Jocelyn's room.

Jeff looked at Jocelyn and she had a look of disbelief on her face. Jeff nodded toward the door, but Jocelyn didn't say anything. She just held a finger up to her mouth to keep him quiet. The person finally left but neither of them was in the mood to continue. Jeff was no longer hard, so he pulled out and stood up.

"Who was that in your room?" Jeff asked.

"It was Monique. I don't know why she stayed there so long though," Jocelyn answered.

"You think she heard us?" Jeff asked.

"I don't care," Jocelyn answered.

Jocelyn began to get dressed so Jeff followed her lead. Jocelyn wanted to check the room and see if anything was missing. Jocelyn wouldn't really know if anything was missing because her mother redid the room about two years ago. She was very curious about why Monique was up there, and she intended to ask.

Jocelyn looked at Jeff and apologized. "I'm sorry baby. We'll finish this later."

"OK. No problem." Jeff answered.

"I know it has been a bunch of stopping and starting, but I will make it up to you," Jocelyn told Jeff as she wiped the sweat off his forehead and kissed him.

"I was definitely not disappointed at what happened here, a little surprised but not disappointed," Jeff told her.

"Well, there's plenty more where that came from," Jocelyn said with a wink. "Are you ready to go back outside?" Jocelyn asked, checking him out to make sure everything was in order.

She thought about what her parents would think if everything wasn't in order. She looked at herself in the mirror, fixing her ponytail and clothes. She looked around to see if she could see anything missing but didn't. She looked at herself and at Jeff once more before they headed back outside.

As soon as she came out Monique came up to them.

"Where were you guys?" She asked. "I was calling you in the house to see if you wanted to play spades, but I couldn't find you, so I got the playing cards and came back out," Monique said.

"I was giving Jeff a tour. You probably just missed us. Did you check in the basement?" Jocelyn asked to play it off.

She was relieved to know that all Monique took was playing cards.

"You know damn well I ain't going in no one's basement," Monique told Jocelyn with a smile. "Do you want the next game?" She asked them.

Jocelyn declined, telling Monique she would catch up with her later. She told her Jeff had work to do so he needed to go home. Jocelyn looked in the driveway and saw Terrell's car was still in the driveway, so she asked Monique where he was.

"I don't know where he went. Lawanna was here earlier so maybe he went down to her house," Monique told Jocelyn.

"Really? So why didn't he move his car?" Jocelyn asked. "My car is in the garage." Jocelyn asked. She didn't know why she was asking Monique that, but she just wanted to go.

Jocelyn looked at Jeff and told him they could go around and say goodbye to her family. She told him, "Maybe Terrell will be back by then. He possibly just went to take his son home."

They said their good-byes and walked around the yard one more time. Jocelyn wrapped her arms around her father's shoulders and kissed him on the cheek. He held Jocelyn there and told her he loved her, and he liked Jeff. He looked up at Jeff and waved goodbye. Jeff came closer and shook his hand. Jocelyn's father told them not to be strangers.

Jocelyn looked in the driveway and saw what she dreaded. Terrell's car was still there. She told Jeff to hold on while she went to get him. He said OK and asked if she needed him to go with her. She said, "No. I should only be a minute. Lawanna lives a few houses down," before she walked off.

When Jocelyn got to Lawanna's house, Lawanna was sitting on the porch.

"Is there something I can help you with?" Lawanna asked Jocelyn, suspiciously.

"Yeah, is Terrell here?" Jocelyn asked.

"Why?" Lawanna asked. She looked Jocelyn up and down but didn't say anything else to her.

"Because Terrell's car is in my driveway, I can't get out of the garage."

Jocelyn answered. She sensed Lawanna's attitude but wasn't going to bait her.

"Terrell is putting his son to sleep, so you are going to have to wait," Lawanna told Jocelyn. "You know he has responsibilities now."

"I understand. I shouldn't have let him park there in the first place," Jocelyn answered. "Do you have keys to his car? Maybe you can move it?"

"Are you trying to be funny? You of all people know Terrell would never let anyone drive his car," Lawanna responded.

Jocelyn could hear the anger in her voice, so she just told her to ask him to come move it when he finished with his son.

Jocelyn walked off bewildered. She didn't understand what Lawanna's problem was. Jocelyn thought, it's not like I slept with her man. She shook it off and went back to explain to Jeff that they would have to wait for Terrell to put his son to sleep. They sat on the front porch because Jocelyn didn't feel like going back into the yard.

"What's on your mind sweetheart?" Jeff asked.

"I am just trying to figure out why Lawanna was so mean to me. I didn't do anything to her," Jocelyn told him. "She made it a point to tell me, 'He has responsibilities now'."

"Maybe she is feeling a little insecure about how it all went down?" Jeff asked.

"Possibly, but there is no need to be mean to me. I don't want Terrell," Jocelyn answered.

Jocelyn didn't want to talk about it anymore. She laid her head in Jeff's chest and pretended to be asleep. Sometime during her pretending, she must have really fallen asleep. Jeff woke her up and told her that Terrell still hadn't moved the car. He told her to come on and took her back up to Lawanna's house. When Lawanna saw them coming, she went into the house and closed the door.

"Lawanna, can you tell Terrell to move the car now!" Jocelyn told her.

"If you wake up my baby you are going to have more problems than just needing a car moved," Lawanna answered through the door.

Jeff banged on the door and told Lawanna to open it.

"I'm going to call the cops if you don't get away from my house," Lawanna told them. "I told him, and he will move it when he is ready."

"No, he won't. He'll move it now or the tow truck will move it," Jeff yelled through the door.

"Um, who the hell are you and what makes you think what you say matters? I could care less if you have his car towed!" Lawanna yelled back.

Jocelyn asked Jeff for his cell phone. She called Terrell's cell phone and he answered.

"Hello?"

"Terrell, can you come move your car please. Now!" Jocelyn demanded.

"Sure. Why are you so angry? Is everything ok?" Terrell asked.

"I asked Lawanna to tell you to move it over an hour ago, but she obviously didn't tell you," Jocelyn stated. "Did she tell you?" She then asked.

"Naw. You know I wouldn't have a problem moving it. I must have fallen asleep when I was putting my son to sleep. I will be right there," Terrell said.

Jocelyn could hear Lawanna arguing with Terrell when he came downstairs. Finally, he told her to shut the hell up before she woke TJ up and opened the door to leave. Lawanna threw something at him and told him, "Next time don't have your bitches coming to my house, disrespecting me."

Terrell was surprised to see Jocelyn and Jeff standing on the porch.

"Why are you here?" Terrell asked.

"I told you I came and asked her about an hour ago. I didn't call your cell phone then because I didn't want it to wake your son and she said she would tell you," Jocelyn explained.

"Get the hell off my property. All of you! Yeah, you too Terrell. Don't come here looking for none later either," Lawanna said.

"Stop playing games, Lawanna. You know damn well we don't be sleeping together and don't wake my son up because I'm not coming back," Terrell told Lawanna.

He then turned to Jeff and Jocelyn and said, "My bad Joce, I didn't know you were in the garage. Why y'all leaving so early?"

"I am tired, and he has work to do," Jocelyn told Terrell.

"Oh, really man? What do you do?" Terrell asked Jeff.

"I'm a lawyer," Jeff answered.

Jocelyn could almost feel him stick his chest out.

"That's cool. Joce, your mom must be happy you got a lawyer?" Terrell asked. "I know she always wanted you to be with a rich man."

Terrell started laughing but Jeff and Jocelyn didn't see anything funny about that statement.

"Seriously Joce, you deserve a good man that can take care of you—even if you don't need it," Terrell said.

Jocelyn shot him a surprised look. She really wished he would shut up and walk the rest of the way in silence.

"Thank you, Terrell. I hope you find someone one day also unless you already have. If that is the case, I wish you well," Jocelyn answered.

It was Terrell's turn to look surprised. He thought that sounded like an answer to the question he asked her earlier. Could it be possible Jocelyn didn't love him anymore? He refused to believe it but that is what that statement had written all over it. Jocelyn got the silence she wanted. Terrell didn't say another word; he didn't even look back at them. He moved the car and beeped the horn as he drove off.

Chapter 10

When Jocelyn reached her house, she asked Jeff if he wanted to come in. She was tired and really just wanted to sleep, but she thought it was only fair to ask him if he wanted to come in. To her surprise, Jeff declined. He told Jocelyn he had a lot of work that needed to be completed and he would call her tomorrow when he cleared some of the work off of his desk.

Jocelyn said OK, but now she was suspicious about his reasons for not wanting to come in. She wondered if he was going start acting funny because they had sex. Jocelyn wondered if she slept with him too soon. She looked up at him and nodded to let him know she understood his reason for not wanting to come in. She didn't though.

Jeff kissed her on the forehead and told her to get some sleep because she looked exhausted. He grinned at her and kissed her on the mouth.

"You are so full of surprises. Thank you for today. All of it," Jeff told Jocelyn. "Your family is very nice."

"I'm glad you had fun. You did have fun, didn't you?" Jocelyn asked. She looked up at him almost pleadingly.

"What's wrong, baby?" Jeff asked after noticing the expression on Jocelyn's face.

"Nothing. You're right. I'm tired," Jocelyn answered.

"Naw, there's something on your mind. Come on, let's go in and talk about it," Jeff responded.

He didn't know what was bothering her, but he wasn't going to leave her without finding out. He thought if it was something he did and he let her sit and think about it, he would pay for it later. He took the keys out of Jocelyn's hand and walked to the house with her.

"I told you I am ok," Jocelyn told him.

"I believe you, but I never want to be too busy to sit and talk to you. No work is worth that," Jeff told her.

Jocelyn looked up at him again. She hoped in her mind Jeff was for real because she was beginning to fall for him and it would be devastating to find out he wasn't real. She forced a smile through her tiredness and Jeff smiled back at her. He opened her front door and held it open for her.

He walked Jocelyn over to her couch and she perked up long enough to tell him not to sit on her couch. She knew Jeff had to smell like smoke because she remembered how her father used to smell after a cookout. He looked surprised when Jocelyn told him not to sit. He understood it when she explained. He told her he would be right back, he had workout clothes in his car he could put on.

When he returned to the house Jocelyn was sitting on the couch. He thought about it and then said, "Hey, why do you get to sit on the couch? You were right there with me when I was cooking, and we also were very close in the house."

"I don't smell like smoke though," Jocelyn tried to justify it.

She knew she probably did but she was so tired she just wanted to sit or lay down.

"Come on," Jeff told Jocelyn. He was headed toward the stairs.

"Where are we going?" Jocelyn asked.

"Upstairs to the tub and that bath stuff you used on me the other night," Jeff answered with a smile on his face.

"I'll never make it up there." Jocelyn said this mostly because she remembered what happened the last time, they were in the tub together.

Jeff came over to the couch and picked Jocelyn up. He carried her up the stairs and put her in the chair in her bedroom. He asked for instructions about using the bath oils and filling up the tub. Jocelyn gave in because she knew there was no way out. She knew she had opened a can of worms by sleeping with Jeff. Now he'll want it all the time, she thought.

Jeff brought Jocelyn a robe from the bathroom. He told her she could put that on while he handled the tub. Jeff saw candles around the tub. He smiled as he thought of Jocelyn lounging in the tub with candles surrounding her. He decided to light them. They smelled like the bath oils. Jeff thought this was funny, but he liked it.

Jocelyn heard Jeff laugh and asked him about it. He told her it was nothing. He told her that her bath would be ready in a minute. He asked Jocelyn if she could put some music on. She asked what he wanted to hear.

"Whatever you listen to when you are in here by yourself," Jeff answered.

Jocelyn thought his request was weird, but she obliged. She put a couple of CDs in the CD player and put the player on shuffle. Jeff heard the music and smiled. He told Jocelyn she could come in and she shuffled into the bathroom. She looked around in amazement.

"Shall I leave you to your bath, madam?" Jeff asked.

"No, you can stay and join me," Jocelyn answered.

Jeff couldn't help smiling at Jocelyn. He began taking off his clothes, pausing to see her reaction. He didn't want to make Jocelyn feel uncomfortable.

Jeff got in the tub and splashed Jocelyn. He laughed when she jumped. She was starting to doze off and her eyes were closed. She told him that it wasn't funny, and he told her he only wanted to alert her to the fact he was in the tub. Jocelyn told Jeff she still didn't think it was funny.

"Come here," Jeff told Jocelyn. "Let me rub your back. I promise I'll behave."

"You better," Jocelyn told him.

Jocelyn scooted over in the tub and Jeff began to rub her back. It felt so good, and she started to relax. Jeff began rubbing lower on her back and on her arms. Jocelyn felt so relaxed that she was getting sleepy. She was about to doze off when Jeff interrupted her.

"So, what was bothering you? Are you still thinking about Lawanna and Terrell?" Jeff asked.

"No. I was thinking about us," Jocelyn answered.

"Thinking about us made you sad?" Jeff asked confused by this. "Did I do something?"

"No, you have been great. I just thought maybe I made a mistake when I had sex with you earlier," Jocelyn answered.

"Why would you think that was a mistake? Did you not want to have sex?" Jeff was still confused.

"No, I did, but I thought maybe it was too soon," Jocelyn answered.

Jeff told Jocelyn he didn't believe in too soon and he felt that if two people are feeling it, they should do it. He thought about his answer and realized it was probably not what Jocelyn wanted to hear. She turned to face Jeff and kissed him. Jocelyn felt Jeff respond to her kiss the same way he did the last time. This time she didn't back away.

Jeff began to apologize but Jocelyn put her finger over his mouth. She began to move away from him, and he thought uh-oh here we go again until she motioned for him to come to her. Jeff crawled across the tub on his hands and knees. He got as close as he could to Jocelyn. She turned Jeff to turn around and sit. He did and she began to rub his back.

Jocelyn was exploring his body. She rubbed his arms, chest, and came back to his shoulders. Jeff took Jocelyn's hands and put them under the water with his. He wanted her to feel his penis.

Jeff turned and faced Jocelyn. He couldn't take it anymore. He pulled her closer to him and waited for a response. There was none so he continued. They continued. Until Jeff looked at her and saw in her eyes that there was still something wrong with her.

"What's wrong? Do you not want this?" Jeff questioned, looking deep into her eyes, trying to read her expression.

Jocelyn didn't answer Jeff. She looked at him for a minute then pushed him out of the way. She got up and out of the tub, got the robe that she wore in the bathroom and left. Jeff laid back in the tub, totally confused and exasperated. He didn't understand her.

Jeff got out of the tub and dried off with a towel. He threw the towel toward the hamper and walked out of the bathroom naked. Jeff kept going. He walked downstairs naked. He was hoping to catch Jocelyn off guard. When he got downstairs Jocelyn was nowhere to be found so he put on the clothes he had brought in from the car.

After he got dressed, he continued to search for Jocelyn. He called out to her, but she didn't answer. He knew she had to be down here because he heard her come downstairs. He started to head toward the front door when he heard a noise from the kitchen. It was the back door being blown by the wind.

Jeff looked out the back door and Jocelyn was sitting at her picnic table. She was still wearing the robe that she left the bathroom in. Jeff walked up to her and asked her to come into the house. He apologized to Jocelyn and tried to take her by the hand.

He apologized again, "I'm sorry. I didn't mean to upset you. I was only wondering."

"Nothing is wrong with me. I'm not upset. I'm just tired," Jocelyn responded. That wasn't all that was wrong with her, but she didn't know exactly what was wrong so she couldn't tell Jeff what was wrong.

Jeff didn't know what to say to that, but he was a little happy to hear that. He was smiling but decided he should wipe the smile off his face before Jocelyn turned around and saw it. He wondered about her still, but he felt he had asked enough questions tonight. He grabbed Jocelyn by the arm and brought her back into the house.

Jeff started looking around Jocelyn's kitchen for a tea kettle and some tea. Jocelyn shot Jeff a confused look before she asked him what he was looking for. He turned and asked where her kettle and tea were. She told him the kettle was in the cabinet next to the stove and the tea was in the one above the refrigerator.

Jeff looked around confused. He wondered how Jocelyn found anything in her kitchen. He didn't ask, he just made the tea. Jocelyn stood the whole time, watching Jeff. When the tea was finished Jeff brought the tea and Jocelyn into the living room and sat on the couch. He wrapped his arms around her, holding the teacup out in front so she could sit in front of him.

He was curious about what would make Jocelyn go outside in the cold like that, but he wasn't going to ask her that either. She laid back into his arms and he brought the tea to her lips. She drank some and then she spoke.

"I'm sorry," Jocelyn began. "I know you must think I am crazy."

"Why are you sorry?" Jeff asked her.

"I know I am running hot and cold. I understand your confusion," Jocelyn told Jeff. She looked back at him and kissed him.

That kiss was like music to Jeff's ears. He also realized Jocelyn was shaking and knew she was going to be sick. He asked her if she had soup, but she didn't. He asked her if she had a blanket. She told him that there was one in the hall closet. He gave Jocelyn the cup of tea and jumped up to get the blanket.

Jeff stopped and looked at Jocelyn as he walked back to the couch. The more he found out about Jocelyn, the more impressed he was. He decided he had found the woman that he wanted to spend the rest of his life with. He got back to the couch and wrapped the blanket and his arms around Jocelyn. She looked back momentarily at Jeff then sank into his arms. She was feeling the same thing. She decided she was going to just go with it from now on.

Soon after Jocelyn fell asleep, her phone rang. Jeff didn't know what else to do so he picked it up. "Hello," Jeff whispered into the phone.

"Hello. Who is this?" the person on the other end asked.

"Who are you looking for?" Jeff asked.

"I'm looking for Joce," Terrell told Jeff.

"Oh, hey Terrell, she's sleeping. I don't want to wake her because I have a feeling she is going to be sick. I'll tell her you called."

"Sick? Is she ok?" Terrell asked. "She looked fine earlier today."

"I'm not saying she is not ok. I just think she is coming down with a cold or something. Remember she said she was tired earlier?" Jeff hoped that would get Terrell off the scent. He added, "She is right here and if I keep talking, she may wake up." He really just wanted to get Terrell off the phone and out of Jocelyn's life.

"Alright, tell her I called. Oh yeah, trust me, she won't wake up from you talking. She is a very sound sleeper," Terrell said before he hung the phone up in Jeff's ear.

Jeff shook his head. He wondered why Terrell was calling her. He thought to himself that Terrell was going to be trouble, but he wasn't going to let it get to him. He had met his wife and Terrell missed his opportunity. That dude needs to move on like Jocelyn told him earlier, Jeff thought.

Chapter 11

Jeff was upset he had to go away. He asked his boss if there was anyone else who could go on the trip. He explained that his girlfriend was sick and he wanted to take care of her. His boss wouldn't budge. He wanted Jeff to go so he could work on this case. Jeff said OK and asked his boss if there was anything else he needed to do in the office. His boss told him no and he could go pack and check on his girlfriend.

Jeff called Jocelyn before he left the office to see if she needed anything. She said no but told Jeff she would like some soup for lunch. He felt sad to break the news to her that he had to leave town for three days. She moaned through the phone and asked who would take care of her. Jeff apologized and asked if she wanted to come with him.

Jocelyn told Jeff that she was only joking. She would be fine, but she would miss him. She got a beep on her phone, so she asked Jeff if he was on his way to her house. He said yeah and she told him she would talk to him then and she had to take the call. Jocelyn wondered who was on the phone because she had never seen the number before. She thought it was possibly work-related because she had all her calls forwarded to her house.

She picked up the phone and it was Terrell. He said he was calling because Jeff told him she was sick.

"You're not pregnant, are you?" Terrell asked.

Jocelyn started laughing but the laughter turned into a coughing spell that hurt her throat.

"No, I am not pregnant," Jocelyn answered Terrell's question.

"Oh ok. That's good, right?" Terrell tried to make it sound like a question.

"Why do you care?" Jocelyn asked.

"I will always care about you. I thought we were still friends if nothing else," Terrell exclaimed. He then asked, "Are we friends?"

Jocelyn told him they were friends, and that she had a cold.

"Oh, that's what ole boy said," Terrell told Jocelyn.

"When and why did you talk to Jeff?" Jocelyn asked.

"When I called Saturday night. I didn't think he would be there," Terrell answered. "So, you two are pretty serious? He answers the phone?"

"Probably because I was asleep. Other than that, no one answers my phone. I'll have to talk to him about that. What if it was my parents?" Jocelyn thought about it as she said it.

"So, how serious are you?" Terrell asked. "Friend to friend."

"We're getting to know each other. Friend to friend," Jocelyn answered with a grin. "So, how is Lawanna?"

"That's not funny. She is trying to say I can't see my son because of what happened Saturday. I told her I would cut the child support out if she tried that nonsense. The fool told me I couldn't because it automatically comes out of my check. I told her I'd tell the court she told me he isn't mine," Terrell explained.

"Can you do that?" Jocelyn asked. "What's wrong with her anyway?"

"I don't know. I guess you set her off. I don't know why though," Terrell answered.

"I don't know why either. We're not together. Jeff seems to think she is bitter about how things turned out. How did things turn out?"

Jocelyn questioned Terrell.

"They didn't turn out well. I told you we were only together once or twice. I thought she was long over me," Terrell answered. "Why do you want to know?"

"Ahh, because the girl almost attacked me on Saturday. I still have to go around there to see my family," Jocelyn answered quickly.

She made sure Terrell didn't think there was any other reason.

"Terrell, that is Jeff at the door. I will talk to you later," Jocelyn said as she heard the doorbell ring.

"Oh, I thought he would have a key to the house," Terrell answered.

"Ha-ha. Very funny, Terrell! Bye," Jocelyn said.

Terrell said bye and they hung up.

"What took you so long to get to the door? Are you ok?" Jeff asked.

Jocelyn shot Jeff a suspicious look before she ushered him into the house.

"I am not checking on you. I am genuinely concerned," Jeff caught the meaning of her look.

"OK," Jocelyn answered as she walked toward the kitchen with the food Jeff brought her. "So, where are you going?"

"I'm going to Baltimore. Why? Do you want to come?" Jeff inquired. "I'll pack your bag and order you a ticket."

"I can't leave. I still have work to do. Just because they don't want my germs in the office doesn't mean they don't need me," Jocelyn said with a laugh and a cough.

"It was worth a try. I am going to miss you and your germs," Jeff told her.

"Oh yeah, you answered my phone the other night?" Jocelyn asked.

Jeff answered quickly. "Yeah. You were asleep and it was loud. I thought it would wake you up, but Terrell cleared that up. He told me you could sleep through anything."

"He said that?" Jocelyn said with a chuckle. Then she got serious and said, "Honestly, don't answer the phone anymore. What if it had been my parents calling. They like you and all, but they are old-fashioned and would have gotten upset about the implications you answering the phone has."

"No problem. I won't do it again," Jeff answered.

He was confused at her request, but he didn't question it because she used her parents as the excuse.

Jocelyn came over and tried to kiss Jeff. He covered his mouth and told her to stop trying to give him her cold. She backed up and blew him a kiss. She felt bad about being so blunt about the phone and she knew he had good intentions when he answered it. She just didn't want everyone rushing to judgment about the level of their relationship. She wasn't sure where they were going.

"Who is going to check in on you while I am gone?" Jeff asked.

"Nobody. I haven't even told my parents I am sick. You took such good care of me," Jocelyn answered. "I'll be fine and brand new when you return."

"Are you sure?" Jeff asked.

"Yep. I have been taking care of myself for a long time, but I didn't mind you taking care of me," Jocelyn said with a smile.

She blew Jeff another kiss.

"I have to go. Enjoy the soup and the brownies. I will call you when I get to Baltimore," Jeff told her as he walked toward the front door.

"Oooh! Brownies. I will enjoy them, but I'll miss you," Jocelyn told Jeff as he walked out the door.

Later that night, Jocelyn was in the kitchen heating up the rest of the soup when the phone rang. She was surprised to hear Terrell's voice on the other end.

"Twice in one day? I didn't get this much attention when we were together," Jocelyn questioned Terrell.

"Well, I know you are sick. Just wanted to make sure you are well taken care of. I know ole boy is there so I'll make it short." Terrell answered Jocelyn's inquiry.

Before Jocelyn knew it, she had told Terrell that Jeff wasn't there and left town. At that moment she smelled the burning soup. She dropped the phone and made a run for the kitchen. She forgot to tell Terrell she was putting the phone down and could hear him screaming her name.

She got back to the phone and told Terrell what happened. He started laughing, partly in relief.

"I thought something happened to you, girl." Terrell told her.

"Naw, I just burned the soup. Now I have to go get more from the store," Jocelyn told Terrell.

"No. You don't. I'll get you some. What do you want? Chicken Noodle? I always heard that it is good for a cold," Terrell said with a grin.

"You don't have to do that. I am feeling much better and some air will do me good," Jocelyn answered Terrell quickly.

She really wasn't feeling better and the thought of going to the store made her stomach turn. But she looked a mess and didn't want him to see her like that. She thought about it: Terrell was her ex-boyfriend, why should she care how she looks to him? With that thought she took Terrell up on his offer but asked if he could find a restaurant that makes soup because she didn't feel like standing up watching it.

"No problem, Joce. Give me a half hour," Terrell answered Her request. "So, chicken noodle is good?"

"Yes. That or Chinese Hot and Sour soup with chicken in it," Jocelyn answered.

They were about to hang up when Jocelyn interrupted Terrell.

"Terrell!" She said into the phone just before he hung up.

"Yep. Do you need something else?" He asked.

"Some juice but that is not why I called your name," She answered. She continued, "Thank you."

"You're welcome. It's not a problem," Terrell answered.

They hung up the phone and Jocelyn smiled at the thought of Terrell doing this for her. It was like pulling teeth to get him to do something for her when they were together. She stopped smiling in mid-thought. She didn't want to take a trip down memory lane. It didn't matter anyway because she and Jeff were happy.

Terrell arrived at her house over an hour later. Jocelyn didn't get mad, she just chalked it up to Terrell being Terrell.

"Sorry it took so long, my mother realized she needed something from the store when she saw me leaving the house. I got her stuff and took it back to the house," Terrell began to explain.

"You're not late. This is not a date or anything," Jocelyn answered. "Thank you for doing this for me."

"No problem. My mother says hi," Terrell told her. "Oh yeah, she told me to tell you she hopes everything is going good between you and that handsome man she saw you with." Terrell began laughing.

"Why are you laughing?" Jocelyn asked him.

He answered through the laugh, "That was my mother's way of reminding me that you're not single."

Jocelyn started laughing with him. She thought to herself, Terrell's mother probably told him that because she was happy to see me with anyone but her son. She always thought I didn't take good enough care of her son. I still don't know what that means but whatever.

"You didn't get yourself something to eat?" Jocelyn asked. She felt odd eating in his face, but she was hungry.

"Naw, my mom cooked earlier and I ate. I am still full. I don't understand why she cooks like that still. It's just me and her now," Terrell answered.

"She is taking care of her baby boy," Jocelyn answered. She hoped Terrell didn't hear the sarcasm in her voice.

He did and responded, "What does that mean?"

"I still don't know. She always told me I didn't take care of you. She probably won't ever think any woman will take care of you like she does," Jocelyn answered. She looked at Terrell and continued, "And you know what? No woman probably will ever take good enough care of you in her eyes."

"Don't worry about her eyes. It's my eyes that count," Terrell shot back. "I know she spoils me, but I also know the difference between my wife and my mother."

Jocelyn just looked at Terrell. She didn't know how to respond to that. She began to talk, "So is that what you are looking for now? A wife?"

"I damn sure ain't looking for my mother," Terrell answered. "Yeah, I am ready to settle down. I hope I didn't let my wife pass me by."

"You can't," Jocelyn answered. "If it is meant to be, it will be."

"I'll try to keep a positive attitude about it, but it's not looking good for me." Terrell told Jocelyn.

"Why do you say that?" Jocelyn asked.

"Because she is with someone else?" Terrell stared at Jocelyn when he answered her question.

He didn't stop staring at her when he stopped talking. He wanted to get a read of her expression.

Jocelyn didn't know what to say to Terrell's declaration. She got up and walked away from the chair she was sitting in. She went into the kitchen and began pouring the juice into a glass. She looked back into the living room and Terrell was looking right at her.

"Do you want some of this juice?" Jocelyn raised the bottle as she asked.

"Naw. You know what? I'm going to go. I have to get up for work tomorrow and I know you need your rest," Terrell answered, realizing how nervous he was making Jocelyn. "Night Joce, I'll talk to you later."

Jocelyn said good night and watched Terrell walk out of the house.

When he left. She sat down in a chair in the kitchen. She was bewildered by Terrell's confession. She felt like she had been sideswiped by a truck. Why was he doing this now, she thought. She knew exactly why Terrell was doing that: because she was with someone else and happy. She told herself she would ignore Terrell's declaration and he would not get to her.

Chapter 12

Jeff went straight to Jocelyn's house from the airport. He was extremely worried about her because she hadn't answered any of his phone calls. They hadn't had a fight and there was no reason to think she wouldn't be speaking to him. He rang the doorbell and got no answer. He walked around the house and saw her car was in the garage. He was truly perplexed at what he could have done to Jocelyn.

Jocelyn heard the bell ring, but she didn't want to talk to anyone. She hadn't answered her phone or talked to anyone since Terrell dropped his bomb on her. She didn't understand why he would say that and why now. She was trying to figure out why it was affecting her the way it was. She looked out her upstairs window and saw Jeff was the one ringing her bell. She wasn't going to answer it at first, but after thinking about it she decided to answer. She didn't want him to alert her family thinking there was something wrong.

She quickly freshened up and did something to her hair. She put on some sweats and answered the door. When she answered Jeff gave a confused look.

"Sorry it took me so long to answer the door. I was in the shower," Jocelyn told Jeff, hoping that would suffice. The look on Jeff's face did not change so Jocelyn continued, "I answered the door when I looked out the window and saw that you were still outside." Jocelyn then threw her arms around Jeff.

Jeff questioned Jocelyn, "How are you baby? Are you feeling ok? I have tried calling you for the past couple of days, but you didn't answer."

"Yeah. I didn't really feel like talking to anyone. I didn't feel great and thought the rest would do me good. I felt a little better when I woke up this morning. I think it is because I knew my baby was coming home today," Jocelyn told Jeff, still watching the look on his face.

Jeff smiled at the thought, but he knew something was not right with Jocelyn.

Jocelyn continued, "I am so happy to see you, but I thought you would go home first."

"I told you I was worried sick about you. Don't ever do that again. Always talk to me, even if it is to say you don't feel like talking," Jeff started.

Jocelyn cut him off. "I'm sorry. I guess I got used to being alone and not having to answer to anyone. I have always taken my time-outs."

Jocelyn figured there was only one way to get him off the subject. She began kissing him. He tried to pull away and talk but Jocelyn wouldn't let him. She began undressing him and he just went with it. He knew they needed to talk but he was so happy to know things are good between them. They made love right there in the doorway. Jeff was as shocked as he was happy.

Jocelyn figured Jeff would forget about what he wanted to talk about, but he didn't. After they made love and were laying together Jeff asked. "Was it something I did?"

"What?" Jocelyn asked. She was thrown off by his question.

"The reason you needed the time-out? Did I cause it?" Jeff asked.

Jocelyn answered it wasn't and began kissing Jeff again, then she turned to him and spoke. "As a matter of fact, it is something you did and are doing. I am falling so hard for you and it's a little scary."

Jeff was surprised and happy. He'd wanted to propose to Jocelyn for about two weeks, and her admission led him to believe it was time.

He figured he would just have to pick the right moment.

"As much as I would like to lay here with you all day and possibly make love to you again, I have to go," Jeff said sadly.

"Go? Was it something I said?" Jocelyn asked.

"No, not at all. I haven't even checked in with the office. I'll come back later tonight," Jeff said as he got dressed.

"OK, I'll be here," Jocelyn answered him. "Later, huh?"

Jeff answered later and kissed Jocelyn on the forehead and then on the lips before he dashed for the door. He was feeling good and decided he was going to propose that night. He had to check in at work and at home, and then he would go out to look for a ring. He was having a hard time believing this, but he was not nervous. He had been looking for a woman like Jocelyn his whole life.

Jocelyn laid on the couch after Jeff left. She did love him, but her behavior the past few days proved to her that she still had feelings for Terrell. She really didn't know what to do about her feelings for Terrell or if anything needed to be done. Jocelyn picked up the phone to call Terrell. She figured talking to him would shed some light on the situation.

"Hello," the voice on the other end answered. Jocelyn was startled because it was a woman's voice.

"Hello?" Jocelyn questioned the person on the other end.

Then she thought about it and decided she must have dialed the wrong number. "I actually think I dialed the wrong number. Sorry to bother you."

"Yeah, you did dial the wrong number. Don't call my man

again," Lawanna answered Jocelyn's confusion.

"Your man?" Jocelyn asked as she caught on to the voice on the other end.

"Yeah, we decided to try and make it work for the sake of our son. Please don't interfere with this," Lawanna told Jocelyn. "I thought you didn't want him anymore now that you have your little lawyer boyfriend?"

"I don't want Terrell. I'm just calling to thank him for the other night," Jocelyn told Lawanna. She knew how it sounded, but she felt Lawanna deserved to wonder.

"Oh yeah? Are you feeling better?" Lawanna asked. She was letting Jocelyn know she knew what happened the other night.

"Yes, thank you." Jocelyn answered, trying to hide her surprise. She was wondering what Terrell told Lawanna and why.

"I would like to thank you for whatever you said to Terrell. Whatever it was, it seems to have Terrell seeing the big picture and how much TJ and I mean to him," Lawanna continued to dig.

"Anything I can do to help Terrell, I'll do. All I want is for him to be happy and if you make him happy, I am happy for you guys." Jocelyn proclaimed. "Tell Terrell I called and thank him for me, ok?" Jocelyn hung up the phone before Lawanna could say anything else. That was completely out of left field, but she could be happy for him if it was for the right reasons. She was having a hard time believing it though. Then she thought, anything could be possible because of the conversation they'd had the other night. She really needed to talk to Terrell now.

Jocelyn unconsciously called Terrell's mother's house and was surprised by him answering the phone.

"Hey," Jocelyn answered after Terrell said hello.

"What a surprise. Are you feeling better? Do you need anything?" Terrell asked.

"I was until I spoke to Lawanna, and she told me you and she got back together." Jocelyn was surprised at her response but not as surprised as Terrell.

"What the hell are you talking about? Are you delusional?" Terrell asked Jocelyn.

Jocelyn answered him by telling him that she'd called his cell phone and about the conversation she had with Lawanna.

"Damn! I asked her if my cell phone was in her house, and she told me it wasn't. I'm sorry. I see she is the one who is delusional." Terrell laughed at the thought.

Jocelyn didn't know exactly how to take Terrell's tale or why she cared. She thought to herself that she did know why she cared. She cared because Terrell had just got through telling her he loved her a couple of nights ago, and the whole situation was confusing her. Terrell brought her out of her thoughts, asking her exactly that—why she cared.

"I don't really care. I just called to see if you are ok. You left my house on a negative note, and I didn't know how to take it," Jocelyn answered.

"It's nice to see you care," Terrell told Jocelyn.

Jocelyn shook her head. It was like he hadn't even heard what she'd said—that she didn't care.

"Well, I'll leave you to handle your girlfriend and get your phone back." Jocelyn laughed at Terrell's predicament.

"Naw, she can have the phone. I'll turn it off and get a new one and she's not even getting the number," Terrell responded to Jocelyn's intended joke and then continued by saying, "You can have the phone number though."

"I won't need it, but what about the rest of your girls? She has access to them, and you know she is going to take full advantage of that."

"Other girls, what other girls? There is no one I care about. The only woman I care about is you, so whatever she wants to do, let her do." Terrell answered. Jocelyn noticed his voice got serious so she thought she would lighten it back up.

"Ok, Terrell. If you say so," Jocelyn quickly retorted.

Terrell sucked his teeth at Jocelyn's blow off and told her, "I know you don't believe me or have any reason to believe but I hope I'll get the chance to prove it to you. I know what I want now, and I will apologize every day for the past if need be. I love you and I know we'll be together."

Jocelyn told Terrell she had to go. She told him Jeff was coming over and she needed to find something to wear. She did this mainly to remind him about Jeff and the fact that she was in a relationship. She wished him well and told him she would talk to him later, hung up the phone and let out a sigh. She was more confused than when she picked up the phone and wondered what Terrell was up to and why he was pulling this now.

Jeff was proud of himself and the ring he picked out for Jocelyn. He just hoped she liked it as much as he did. It was expensive but it was an expense Jeff was willing to incur. He hoped he would only have to do this once in his life. He was feeling confident after the time he'd spent with Jocelyn that day, and hoped he felt the way he felt right now for the rest of his life.

Jocelyn sat nervously waiting for Jeff to get there. She hoped she wouldn't act indifferent toward him because of the situation with Terrell. Damn him for springing this on her right now, she thought. She attempted to clear her head of all thoughts of Terrell, but it wasn't working. She told herself the only reason that Terrell was doing this now was because of her relationship with Jeff. She just knew he couldn't be serious.

There was a time when Jocelyn would have died to hear Terrell say he loved her or talk about the future with her. She thought to herself she couldn't risk it right now. Things with Jeff were too good. She sat quietly, thinking about Jeff, their relationship, and concluded she was where she wanted to be. Theirs was the most stable relationship Jocelyn had ever been in and she liked how it felt. She realized at that moment, this was what she had searched for her whole life and told herself she was going to see it through.

Jocelyn was startled out of her thoughts by the doorbell. She opened it and immediately threw her arms around Jeff. Jeff was surprised but appreciative. He was holding a couple of bags of groceries. He quickly dropped them to pick Jocelyn up and kiss her after her warm welcome. Jocelyn noticed the bags and became curious.

"What are those?" Jocelyn asked.

"Dinner?" Jeff responded smiling. "I hope you don't mind staying home tonight."

Jocelyn was relieved. "Nope, not at all. I actually prefer it."

"Good, because I am going to make my specialty—grilled Cajun-style salmon with curried rice and vegetables," Jeff answered with a smile.

Jocelyn looked at Jeff and let out a laugh. "That's your specialty? Most people say spaghetti or something like that. Do you need anything from me?"

Jeff shook his head to alert Jocelyn to the fact that she would not be needed and headed for the kitchen.

"What am I supposed to do while you are cooking?" Jocelyn asked.

"Rest and relax, but whatever you do, do not come in here," Jeff yelled from the kitchen.

Jocelyn laid on the couch and wondered what Jeff was up to. She was grateful he wanted to cook dinner because her mind was definitely not on cooking. She thought about him telling her not to come into the kitchen. The more she thought about it, the more she wanted to get up and go into the kitchen. She started to get up and as if he'd heard her move, Jeff came to the kitchen door.

"Would you like something to drink? I brought some white wine to go with dinner, but I'll make an exception for you and give you some before dinner." Jeff winked at Jocelyn.

"Give me some before dinner? Are you coming on to me?" Jocelyn answered.

Jeff shook his head and told Jocelyn not to tempt him. He told her he would have to change the name of the recipe to blackened Salmon and for her not to come over there. They both laughed and Jeff ducked back into the kitchen.

Jocelyn's phone rang. She deliberated long and hard but then decided to answer it. The call was private, so she was very hesitant. She figured Jeff would think there was something wrong or she was trying to hide if she didn't answer it, so she did. Terrell was on the other end. Jocelyn asked him why he was calling and asked him to call her another time. He told her that was fine and that he was only calling to leave his new phone number on her answering machine.

"What are you doing at home? Your boyfriend is a big-time lawyer, couldn't he spring for dinner?" Terrell asked.

"He is in the kitchen cooking. He said he wanted to stay in," Jocelyn answered quickly.

"I bet he would. He hasn't been in town for a few days," Terrell insinuated.

Jocelyn caught his insinuation but didn't dignify it with an answer. Her first impulse was to tell him they took care of that earlier that day, but she didn't. She figured there was no reason to rub Terrell's face in it.

Terrell spoke again, "I'm sorry. That was out of line. Do you want the number?"

"Yeah, I'll take the number," Jocelyn answered. She wondered why she didn't just say no, and she really wanted to get Terrell off the phone before Jeff came back out.

Terrell gave her the number and warned her not to do anything he wouldn't do. He told her he loved her and wished her a good night before he hung up. Jocelyn set the phone down and just stared at it. She really didn't know why she still talked to Terrell. She was going to put a stop to it. The next time he called she wouldn't answer. Being friends with him was not a good thing at this point in her life.

Jeff called Jocelyn into her dining room. She looked at him after she saw he had set the table up and even put candles out. She questioned, "What's for dessert? And where did you get candles?" She saw the small plates with aluminum covers on them, which was usually used for dessert. Jeff told her not to touch those and it was a surprise. She smiled a devious grin at Jeff but then agreed not to touch the plates. She couldn't believe he went through all that work.

Jeff came over and pulled her chair out for her and pushed her back toward the table. Jeff then went to the other side of the table and sat down. He instructed her to take the aluminum cover off the big plate only. She smiled at him again and obeyed. She was extremely curious to know what was under the smaller plate at this point. She didn't smell anything sweet cooking, but he could have bought something. She hoped it was cheesecake.

They ate in utter silence. Jeff was so nervous that he thought that if he spoke, he would reveal what he was up to or mess up the moment. Jocelyn spoke once halfway through the meal to let Jeff know how good the food was. It was good too. Jocelyn could definitely be happy with a man who cooks like this. She wondered, though, if he would continue to cook as time went on. They were still in the stage of the relationship where they tried to impress each other.

Jeff rose when he finished eating. He asked Jocelyn if she was done eating and she nodded that she was. He picked up her plate and carried it to the kitchen. He returned and told her she could lift the aluminum top off the smaller plate.

"I really don't feel like eating dessert. I am so full." Jocelyn playfully stated.

"OK. I'll just take this away," said Jeff.

He scooped the plate up and began to clear it from the table. Jocelyn grabbed him by the arm. Her curiosity was too much for her to keep up the game. She had to know what was under the cover.

"What's under here?" Jocelyn asked.

"Don't worry. I'll just put it up for later," Jeff answered.

Jeff was glad her curiosity was getting the best of her because he didn't actually have any dessert for her.

"No, I'll eat it now," Jocelyn answered quickly. "I can eat it."

"Are you sure?" Jeff questioned. "I don't want to force you."

"No. Give it to me." Jocelyn was practically begging.

Jeff sat the plate back on the table and backed away. Jocelyn lifted the cover and saw the box it contained.

"What's this?" Jocelyn asked. She looked up at Jeff for an answer.

"Open it." Jeff answered.

Jocelyn opened the box and her mouth dropped. She couldn't speak. She turned to look at Jeff as he dropped to one knee and proposed.

When he finished, he looked up to see Jocelyn nodding her head. She was nodding yes, but the word hadn't come out of her mouth.

"I can't hear you," Jeff broke the silence.

Jocelyn grabbed him around his neck and screamed, "Yes! Yes, I will marry you!"

"Are you sure?" Jeff asked.

"Yeah, I'm sure. I have never been so sure of anything in my life," Jocelyn answered.

This shocked Jeff. He didn't expect her to say no, but he also didn't expect her to be so sure of it. He took her in his arms and held her.

"I have a confession to make," Jeff started.

Jocelyn began to get worried. What could he possibly have to confess, she thought. So, she asked. "What?"

"There isn't any dessert," Jeff answered with a grin.

"Oh! I can live with that confession," Jocelyn told him and laughed.

"What did you think? I was going to tell you I was a cross dresser or had a couple of kids stashed around the country?" Jeff asked.

"I've heard worse," Jocelyn answered.

Jocelyn couldn't believe this was happening. This was definitely what she had been looking for and waiting for her whole life. Jeff was stable, had no children, had a good job, a sense of family, and all the other things Jocelyn had always wanted in a husband. She couldn't wait to tell her parents and everyone. She thought about all the things that would need to be done, all the planning. She was so far ahead she was already at the wedding when Jeff interrupted her thoughts.

"Can I come?" Jeff asked when he saw the blissful look on Jocelyn's face.

"You mean you aren't there with me? I thought we were both happy about this?" Jocelyn questioned.

"I am definitely there. I just wanted to make sure you are in the same place I am. You have made me a very happy man," Jeff told Jocelyn. He kissed her on her forehead and then on the lips before he began to talk again. "So, where are we going to get married and when?"

Jocelyn began to think. Damn that was one thing she hadn't envisioned—the date.

"Do you have a date in mind?" Jocelyn asked.

"As soon as possible?" Jeff answered.

"Not too soon. There is so much that needs to be done," Jocelyn mumbled.

"OK, whenever you are ready." Jeff answered. "I am leaving it in your capable hands."

Jocelyn let Jeff know he was going to be a big part of the planning and would not get away with "just showing up."

"I can't wait to tell my parents," Jocelyn continued.

"Why wait? We can go now," Jeff responded.

Jocelyn looked up at Jeff and shook her head. "Yeah, we can go now."

They got up off the couch and kissed a couple of times. Jocelyn got her coat and then they were off.

Chapter 13

They drove in silence to her parents' house. The silence worried Jeff. He thought she would have more to say; he thought he would have more to say. That was part of the reason he had suggested they go to her parents' house. When they arrived at her parents', Jocelyn grabbed him by the hand and began to swing their hands back and forth as they walked toward the house.

Jeff began to wonder what her parents would say about their engagement. He couldn't imagine them having a problem with it, but he would prepare himself for anything.

Jocelyn's mother answered the door. She had a look of shock on her face. The look was almost alarming.

"What are you doing here?" Mrs. McCrary asked.

"We have good news, Mama," Jocelyn answered.

"By all means, come in. I have to warn you that we have other company," Mrs. McCrary said and stared at Jocelyn.

Jocelyn didn't seem to catch the meaning of the stare or didn't notice it. Jeff noticed it and responded.

"Would you like us to come back at a more convenient time?" Jeff asked.

"No! Nonsense! Anytime is convenient for my daughter and good news," Mrs. McCrary answered and looked back toward Jocelyn.

Jeff was well aware that Jocelyn's mother was attempting to relay something to her, but he couldn't tell whether Jocelyn didn't notice or if she was ignoring her mother. Finally, Mrs. McCrary moved from the doorway and ushered us into the living room. To both of their surprise, Terrell was sitting in there with Mr. McCrary, playing cards. Jocelyn looked up at Jeff and gave him an "I didn't know" look. Jeff kissed her on the forehead to let her know that he understood.

Mrs. McCrary spoke first. She alerted Mr. McCrary to the fact Jocelyn had good news. Mrs. McCrary then turned her attention to Jocelyn and motioned for her to begin. Jocelyn was nervous about Terrell being there. In all her excitement, she hadn't once thought about him or how this would affect him. Well, she guessed she would find out. Without any hesitation she stuck her left hand out and let the diamond sparkle.

Mrs. McCrary jumped out of her seat and ran over to hug her daughter. Mr. McCrary stayed seated and looked at Jeff.

"It was too much for you to ask her father for her hand?" Mr. McCrary started.

"No, not at all Sir. I am sorry. I do admit I forgot because I got caught up in the moment." Jeff responded. He was a little confused at Mr. McCrary's response, but he understood he probably should have asked. Jeff continued, because Mr. McCrary's face hadn't changed. "It would be my honor if you would allow your daughter to marry me. I only asked her first because I wasn't sure she would say yes and didn't want her to feel cornered if you knew and she decided she didn't want to marry me."

Mr. McCrary nodded at Jeff. He could respect what Jeff was saying. "Yeah, you probably thought she might not say yes because it is kind of soon?"

"It is soon, but I am sure I want to marry your daughter. I have searched for someone like her my whole life," Jeff responded.

Mr. McCrary scratched his chin and looked at his daughter. She was beaming and showing the ring to her mother. How could he disagree with anything that makes her smile like that? Mr. McCrary turned to Jeff and told him to look at Jocelyn. He told Jeff that she better smile like that for the rest of her life or Jeff would have to answer to him. Jeff nodded to let Mr. McCrary know he understood, and Mr. McCrary told him he would allow him to marry Jocelyn.

At that moment Terrell got up to go. He told everyone that he saw they were having a family moment before he told Mr. McCrary they could continue their card game another time. He looked at Jocelyn and congratulated her. He couldn't get his eyes to turn away after he said it, so he backed out of the room. He was hoping Jocelyn would come to him, run after him or something. How could she do this after he'd poured out his heart to her, he thought.

Jocelyn's mother continued to ogle over the ring. Jeff finally sat down on the couch and began to speak to Mr. McCrary again. He apologized once more for not asking for Jocelyn's hand and told him how much he loves Jocelyn. Mr. McCrary did nothing but nod. He really didn't know what to say; especially since the conversation he felt he should have had with Jeff he had with Terrell instead. Mr. McCrary was trying to find a way to get Jocelyn alone and tell her. He thought to himself there was no better way than to just do it, so he called his daughter and asked her to follow him into the kitchen.

Jocelyn skipped behind her father unaware of what was in store for her. Her father felt sad but thought his daughter should have this information.

"How's it going sweetheart?" Mr. McCrary started off.

"It's going well. How are you doing, Daddy?" Jocelyn answered.

"I'm good, but a little perplexed. I had an interesting talk with Terrell before you came in." Mr. McCrary hesitated, he was thinking of changing his mind and not telling Jocelyn. "He asked my permission to marry you."

"What? Daddy, what are you talking about? That was Jeff." Jocelyn said. She was startled at what her father was saying.

"No! Jeff didn't ask me first. I do know the difference between them," Mr. McCrary retorted.

"What did you tell Terrell?" Jocelyn inquired.

"I told him I would talk to you about it and get back to him," He responded.

"Why would he do that Daddy?" Jocelyn asked.

"Because he loves you. I asked him the same thing. I told him he needed to be sure. He told me that he was sure. He said he has been talking to you about it." Her father searched Jocelyn's face for a response.

"I didn't take him seriously. I thought he was only trying to get to me because I am in a relationship," Jocelyn answered sadly. "What am I going to do? I would never want to hurt Terrell this bad."

"There is nothing you can do about it now. What's done is done. Just be sure you are making the right decision for you," Mr. McCrary told his daughter. "I'm sorry to tell you this right now, but I didn't want to keep it from you."

"It's ok, Daddy. I'll take care of it. I am sure I made the right decision, though, and I am happy you approve," Jocelyn answered and smothered herself in her father's chest.

Jocelyn and her father came back into the living room just in time. Jocelyn's mother was showing Jeff pictures of Jocelyn when she was small and telling him all the childhood stories she knew. She told him she would give them some of the childhood pictures to put up in their home.

"Where are you going to live?" Mrs. McCrary asked.

"Good question," Jeff answered. "I will get on it right away."

"Honey, you know I own the house I live in right," Jocelyn answered.

"Yes, I figured that, but I want to live in a house that represents both of us. One that we have room for growth in," Jeff responded.

Jocelyn said nothing else. She loved her house and wondered why he figured a three-bedroom house was not one they could grow in. She didn't know how to take it. Redecorating is one thing but she really didn't feel that moving out was necessary. She wondered what else Jeff wanted to change about her life. Jocelyn began worrying about losing her independence.

Jocelyn was getting tired, and the developments of the night had her in a strong state of confusion. Jocelyn wanted to go home.

"I have to get up early in the morning, so I think Jeff and I should call it a night," Jocelyn said, breaking the chatter that was going on between her parents and Jeff.

"Congratulations Joce, Jeff," Mr. McCrary said as they headed toward the door.

Jocelyn began thinking about what her father told her about Terrell. She was really concerned about him. The whole thing was a mess. Jocelyn wondered why she couldn't just be happy, why everything had to be so complicated. She thought about it and knew Terrell didn't do this to spite her. He had no way of knowing Jeff was going to propose. She didn't know who to talk to about this.

She realized she had gotten as much out of her father as she was going to get. She wondered if her mother knew about it. Her mother appeared genuinely happy for her and Jeff, but that didn't mean she didn't know about Terrell. Her mother liked Terrell, but she always thought that Terrell was below Jocelyn and that Jocelyn could do better. Someone like Jeff would definitely please her mother more than Terrell.

The ride home was as quiet as the ride to her parents' house. Jeff took opportunities to sneak looks at Jocelyn; she looked sad. He did this a few times and then he couldn't take it anymore.

"Are you ok?" Jeff asked.

"Yes. Why would you ask?" Jocelyn responded.

"Because you look sad. Was it something your father said?" Jeff continued to question.

Jocelyn looked at Jeff and forced a smile. "No. I'm just tired. I am still getting over my cold."

"OK. I'll let you get some sleep and talk to you tomorrow," Jeff said to Jocelyn.

Jeff knew there was more to the story but decided to leave it alone. To him, Jocelyn was hardly looking like a happy, newly engaged woman. When they reached her house, he walked over to her side of the car and opened the car door for her. He walked her to the door and kissed her on the forehead. Jocelyn responded by grabbing Jeff and hugging him tight.

When Jocelyn let Jeff go, she stared at him and thanked him. She asked if she would see him the next day before she turned and went into the house. Once she was in the house she began to cry. She was crying because she didn't know what to do about Terrell. She didn't want to hurt either of them.

Jocelyn's phone began to ring, and she answered without checking the caller ID. Monique was on the other end. Jocelyn hadn't spoken to Monique in a while, so she figured she could take the time to talk to her now.

"Where have you been hiding?" Monique answered.

"I have been busy, sick, and engaged," Jocelyn answered.

"Did you say engaged? What?" Monique squealed. "To who?"

"To who? Of course, it is Jeff. Who else would I be engaged to?" Jocelyn knew the answer to that.

"Does he know?" Monique's voice got serious.

"Yes." Jocelyn answered. Although they didn't say his name, they both knew who 'he' was. "He was at my parents' house when Jeff and I got there. Monique, he was asking my father for permission to marry me."

"What! Get out!" Monique was going into full gossip mode. "What did he say about you getting engaged to Jeff?"

"Nothing. He sat through it," Jocelyn started. "I had no idea what he was there for, and I would never want to hurt him like that."

"Yeah, but what could you do?" Monique asked.

"I don't know," Jocelyn answered.

She was getting tired of talking about it.

"So, how did you find out Terrell was there to ask your father to marry you?" Monique asked.

"My father told me. So, what's going on with you?" Jocelyn responded and tried to quickly change the subject.

Monique answered, "Apparently nothing compared to what's going on with you."

"Monique, promise me you won't tell anyone about this because I don't want Terrell to think I am happy about what happened." Jocelyn asked Monique to do something she knew she probably wouldn't.

"Fine! Dang, you act like I am always gossiping or something," Monique answered and sucked her teeth at Jocelyn's request.

"I didn't say that. I just want to be sure that no one knows until I see how he is doing with all of this. Can I call you tomorrow? In the morning I am going to work for the first time since being sick and I need to get some sleep," Jocelyn inquired.

"Aight! Good night. Call me tomorrow," Monique answered. Jocelyn said good night to Monique, and they hung up the phone.

Jocelyn reached back to the table for the notebook she had written Terrell's new phone number in earlier that night. She looked at the number but couldn't bring herself to dial it. She really didn't know what to say to him. She finally dialed the number, but Terrell didn't pick up. She dialed it again and got the same thing. She began to worry about Terrell and decided she was going to go see him.

Chapter 14

Jocelyn reached Terrell's mother's house in about 10 minutes. She went up to the door and stood there for about a half hour. She didn't know if she should ring the bell or knock or what. She finally rang the doorbell and waited for someone to answer it. She sat down on the top step and waited. She decided that she wasn't going anywhere until she spoke to Terrell.

Terrell's mother came home and saw Jocelyn sitting on the stairs. She asked Jocelyn, "What is wrong? Why are you here."

Jocelyn looked up at her momentarily and then re-captured her train of thought. "I got engaged tonight," Jocelyn answered.

"Congratulations sweetheart," Terrell's mother told Jocelyn.

"Thanks," Jocelyn responded.

"It still doesn't explain why you are sitting on my front stairs. Terrell should be in the house. I wonder why he didn't open the door." She gave Jocelyn a long, suspicious look.

"Terrell was there when I announced it to my parents. He was there visiting my father, seeking permission to ask me to marry him," Jocelyn continued.

"I always told my son you were going to break his heart one day," She answered.

"I had no idea, and I would never hurt Terrell," Jocelyn shouted at Terrell's mom before she realized what she was doing.

"But you always do. You always hurt him. He is not good enough for you or he's not doing what you want him to do, when you want it done and you're gone. I don't understand why he isn't sick of it yet. Hopefully this will be the motivation he needs to find someone who cares about him." She looked down at Jocelyn and then walked right past her. She didn't invite her in or tell her she would see if Terrell was in the house. Terrell's mother went into the house and slammed the door behind her. Jocelyn was shocked at the attitude Terrell's mother took toward her. She didn't know why though. She'd always hated Jocelyn.

    Jocelyn wanted to leave. She wanted to go home and forget this whole night happened. She got into her car and began to drive but she broke down crying again. She pulled over and parked the car because she knew she couldn't go any further. She leaned on her steering wheel and just balled. She couldn't believe all this drama was happening on what was supposed to be one of the happiest days of her life. She began to think about the whole situation and decided she was going to be happy. She was engaged to a considerate man who loved her and dammit she was going to be happy.

    Jocelyn got up and dried her eyes. She pulled out of the parking spot she was in and drove back home. She was so shaken up, she never noticed Terrell was following her in his car. When she got to her house and got out of the car, he shouted at her.

    "Why were you at my house? You didn't humiliate me enough at your parent's house?" Terrell asked.

    "No! I wanted to make sure you were ok. I had no idea until my father told me later," Jocelyn answered.

    "You had plenty of ideas. I told you how I felt but I guess that doesn't matter to you. You would rather marry someone you barely know because he has money!" Terrell screamed at Jocelyn.

    Jocelyn came back toward Terrell's car in hopes of quieting him down. She could only imagine how many of her neighbors were squinting through their window shades.

    "Terrell, you know that is not true," Jocelyn pleaded with

Terrell.

"It's not? I saw your mother beaming with pride over the big ring her daughter scored! I see what you're about!" Terrell still screamed it.

"Why are you screaming?" Jocelyn asked Terrell.

"Why not? Isn't this the happiest day of your life? Don't you want your neighbors to know that you snagged a big fish?" Terrell continued to scream.

"I'm not going to talk to you if you continue to scream like this," Jocelyn declared and walked back toward her house.

"Yeah, you're right. We don't have anything else to talk about anyway," Terrell answered. "Have a nice life."

"What?" Jocelyn responded. "Just like that? We have nothing to talk about?"

"Yep," Terrell said. "Just like that."

Terrell pulled off and tried to drive away. Jocelyn jumped in front of his car. For a minute or two she didn't think Terrell was going to stop. Terrell was thinking of not stopping. At the last minute he pressed hard on the brakes and came less than an inch away from Jocelyn. Jocelyn stood stiff. Terrell got out of the car and grabbed her. He held her in his arms.

"You know I would never hurt you, right?" Terrell asked Jocelyn.

Jocelyn didn't answer, she didn't move. Terrell held her under her chin and lifted her head to him. He then kissed Jocelyn on the forehead and looked down at her. Jocelyn looked back at Terrell and to his surprise she kissed him. He was so shocked that he tried to pull away. But then he thought about how long he'd waited for this moment, so he pulled Jocelyn back to him and kissed her back. They stood there kissing in the middle of the street until a car came from the other way and the headlights broke the trance.

"What happened here?" Terrell asked Jocelyn. "And why?"

"I don't know what happened. I got engaged tonight. I'm sorry Terrell," Jocelyn said.

"Sorry? What are you saying? You're still going to marry him?" Terrell asked in shock.

"Yes. I said yes to him, and I meant it," Jocelyn responded and looked Terrell right in his eyes.

"But you love me. Tell me you don't," Terrell answered her response.

"I admit I still have feelings for you, but I don't think I love you anymore," Jocelyn told Terrell.

"So why did you kiss me?" Terrell asked.

"I was confused because of what happened. I can't explain it."

"What are you afraid of?" Terrell asked. "Not pleasing your mother? Not being rich? What is making you hold back from us?"

"I'm engaged," Jocelyn answered. "Nothing is holding me back from us because there is no us."

"Yes, there is, and you know it and feel it," Terrell told Jocelyn. He tried to kiss her again, but she pulled away.

Jocelyn went over to Terrell's car and sat on the hood. He watched her in silence and waited for her to say something else. She didn't. They stared at each other for what seemed like an eternity to Terrell. He finally threw his arms in the air to get Jocelyn's attention.

"If there is nothing else, get off my car so I can go home," Terrell told Jocelyn. He didn't even attempt to hide his contempt.

"What?" Jocelyn asked.

"Get off my car and stay out of my life," Terrell said. He didn't mean the second part, but he was going for effect.

"You're the one who is always talking about us being friends. What do you mean stay out of your life?" Jocelyn was appalled at Terrell saying that to her.

"I don't want to be your friend anymore," Terrell said.

"Why? Because you can't have me?" Jocelyn asked.

Terrell got in his car and slammed the door. He started the car and yelled out the window. "Stay there if you want to."

Jocelyn thought for sure that Terrell would not drive off with her on the hood. She was wrong. Terrell began driving slowly and then began picking up speed. Jocelyn shouted for him to stop and told him that she would get off the hood. She got off the hood when he stopped and ran to the driver's side of the car. She stared at Terrell and just began to cry. She backed away from the car and let Terrell drive off.

Jocelyn watched Terrell drive off. She looked around to see how many of her neighbors were watching. She didn't see any, but she knew they were watching. She walked to her house and sat on the front stairs. She couldn't bring herself to go into the house. She didn't mean to hurt Terrell, but she had to marry Jeff. Jocelyn re-lived her and Terrell's past and saw all the break-ups, arguments, and problems and then she looked at her relationship with Jeff, it is as close to perfect as any relationship she had ever had.

Jocelyn was thinking about it and wondering if she really loved Jeff or if she just loved that their relationship was good. They hadn't been dating that long and she still had feelings for Terrell. Jocelyn ran to her car and got in it. She decided to go see Jeff. She had to know tonight if she made a mistake.

When she got to Jeff's apartment building, she stood outside for a while. She couldn't bring herself to knock on the door. She began to walk away but she decided that she needed to do this tonight. She began banging on Jeff's front door. Jeff opened the door and looked at Jocelyn. He asked if she was ok, and she answered that she didn't know. He asked if she knew what time it was, and she didn't know that either. Jeff invited Jocelyn in and told her to sit on the couch.

"Can I get you something baby?" Jeff began. "What are you doing here?"

Jocelyn looked at Jeff and motioned for him to come closer to her. She kissed him and then pulled back.

"Why do you love me?" Jocelyn asked.

"I love you for many reasons. Why do you ask?" Jeff responded.

"What are they?" Jocelyn asked.

"One of them is your unpredictability. I would have never expected to see you at my door tonight or we would be having this conversation hours after I proposed to you." Jeff was a little annoyed with the question. He figured the whole proposing thing would let her know how much he loves her.

"I'm sorry, I'm just trying to figure this out," Jocelyn answered, noticing the annoyance in Jeff's voice.

"Figure out what?" Jeff asked. "You don't love me, do you?"

Jocelyn just stared at Jeff. Hearing it made it all suddenly make sense to her. Terrell was right: she loved the idea of him but not him. She didn't answer Jeff, she didn't move. She couldn't move.

"Answer me, Jocelyn!" Jeff demanded.

"I'm not sure. I love you. I love the thought of you. I love what we have together. I just want to be sure," Jocelyn told him and kissed him again.

"If you're not sure, I got my answer," Jeff told Jocelyn.

"What do you mean?" Jocelyn asked. "Marriage is a big step.

Don't you want to be sure?"

"I am sure," Jeff answered. "I thought you were sure too because you said yes."

"I meant the yes," Jocelyn retorted.

"So, what changed?" Jeff asked.

"Nothing," Jocelyn answered quickly.

"Please don't lie to me. At least have the decency to be honest with me."

"I'm sorry Jeff. It's not you. It's not us," Jocelyn began. "When my father pulled me out of the room tonight-"

"He doesn't like the fact I didn't ask him first." Jeff cut Jocelyn off. "Did he tell you not to marry me?"

"No, it was nothing like that. My father told me the reason Terrell was there when we arrived was because he was asking my father's permission to marry me," Jocelyn stated and looked up at Jeff.

"Why would he think he had a chance at you saying yes to marrying him?" Jeff asked.

"I don't know, but we have been talking lately," Jocelyn answered.

"About marriage?" Jeff asked.

"No!" Jocelyn quickly answered. "He talked about it, but I didn't take him seriously."

Jeff couldn't believe this. He wanted to yell or something. Actually, he didn't, he wanted to fight for his fiancée, but he realized he had already lost. He just stared at her, trying to read her and understand how something that was so right earlier was so wrong now. He thought he should have known it was too good to be true. He knew finding a good woman would never be that easy for him.

"So, what do you want to do?" Jeff asked. He just wanted to end the agony.

"What?" Jocelyn asked.

"What do you want to do? I know you don't want to marry me." Jeff looked at Jocelyn. "Please don't say you do because I don't want second place."

"Second place. You will never be second," Jocelyn answered.

Jeff was frustrated by the whole situation. He told Jocelyn to take all the time she needed to make her decision and get back to him when she decided what she wanted. He motioned for her to get up and gave her a hug before leading her to the door. He knew she wouldn't be back and at this point he didn't care. He would rather she just go and not have to see her again. He didn't even care about the ring. She could keep it.

Jocelyn looked back at Jeff as she left his place. She wanted to go back and change everything she said to him. She just knew she was making the biggest mistake of her life. Her life could be good with Jeff. Love and passion doesn't have the staying power that stability and growth have, does it? She didn't want to go home but there was nowhere else she could go.

She got in her car and drove around for a while and ended up in front of Terrell's mother's house. Terrell's car wasn't there. She wondered where he could be this time of the night. She looked around to make sure he wasn't behind her like last time. She didn't see him. She finally drove off and decided to go home.

Chapter 15

The next day at work, Jocelyn couldn't get any work done. She brought Terrell's cell phone number with her to work and called it three times, but Terrell wasn't answering it. She looked down at her finger and realized she still had her engagement ring on. She didn't know what to do with it. She figured she would eventually have to give it back to Jeff.

She continued to look at the ring and wondered how she got there. Last night she was on top of the world, ready to get married and today she was how she always seemed to end up—alone. She replayed the previous night in her head and began to shake her head. She should have just taken the information her father gave her and stuck it in the back of her mind.

Her receptionist Marie was standing over her when she came to. Marie was pointing at the ring and smiling at her.

"Is that what I think that is?" Marie asked.

"No. It's just a ring. Maybe I should take it off this finger," Jocelyn answered.

"Are you ok?" Marie asked. "I am here for you if you need to talk to someone."

"Thanks, Marie. I am fine" Jocelyn answered. "Wait, do you believe in 'The One'?" Yes, I do. I hope to find him one day. Why do you ask? Have you found yours?" Marie responded.

"Yes, I think I have," Jocelyn answered.

"I knew it! And you tried to tell me it isn't an engagement ring!"

Marie screeched with joy.

"The engagement ring is from someone else. I didn't realize how much I loved the other person until it was too late," Jocelyn answered. She then asked, "Do you think stability and wealth lasts longer than passion?"

Marie looked at her boss like she was ridiculous. She didn't understand why someone who had it going on like Jocelyn would be worried about wealth and stability. She owned her own home, car, and had job stability within her chosen field. She thought only women who didn't have all those things looked for men who had money. Marie tried to figure out a way to inquire about this that wouldn't offend Jocelyn because she was still her boss.

"Why do you care how much money a man makes?" Marie asked.

"I don't really, but everyone wants stability," Jocelyn answered. She thought to herself Marie was indirectly calling her a gold digger.

"Don't you feel you have accomplished enough to marry for love and passion and all that great stuff?" Marie asked and looked at her boss.

"Yes, I do, but it's not all about what I have accomplished. I believe a couple should have plans and hopes as a couple so we both should be accomplished," Jocelyn retorted.

"Well then, go with your beliefs and ignore your heart," Marie told Jocelyn and headed for the door.

Marie left Jocelyn to think about what they'd talked about. She wondered about what Marie must think of her wanting to choose security over love. Jocelyn thought about it more and realized the biggest problem in her relationship with Terrell, and all her other relationships, was worrying about what other people thought about her and her decision to stay with someone or be with someone. It was time for her to forget about everyone else and do what she felt was right in her heart.

Jocelyn picked up the phone and dialed the number Terrell gave her again. He still didn't answer, so she left a message for him to call her. She sent the urgent message and left her work number. She knew he must be mad at her, but she didn't understand why he didn't answer his phone. She wanted him to yell at her, curse her, do something to let her know he was not completely done with her.

Jocelyn's phone began to ring. She looked down and saw it was her mother. She thought to herself, 'What would her mother think of her calling things off with Jeff?' She knew her mother would just keep calling if she didn't speak to her. So, she answered it.

Her mother started right in, "When do you want to start planning your wedding?"

"I don't know Mom. I haven't given it much thought," Jocelyn answered. She wanted to tell her mother, but she didn't want to hear her mother's response. So much for her thoughts of not worrying what anyone thought.

"You don't know? You don't sound like a woman who is newly engaged. Are you sure you are alright?" Jocelyn's mom asked after picking up on Jocelyn's tone.

Before Jocelyn knew what she was doing she said, "No it's not ok. I love Terrell. Jeff and I are not getting married."

"What?" Jocelyn's mother asked. "Where did this come from?"

"Daddy said…." Jocelyn began.

Her mother cut her off. "I can't believe your father would do that. Why would he tell you?"

"What? You knew about Terrell asking to marry me?" Jocelyn asked. "Why did you make such a big deal about Jeff and my engagement in front of Terrell then?" Jocelyn asked her mother. She was shaking her head in disbelief.

"Because Jeff is what you need! I am going to pick the man I believe is better for my baby every time. You can't fault that!" Her mother boomed at her.

"Why is he better, Mommy? Because he makes more money than Terrell?" Jocelyn asked.

Jocelyn's mother sucked her teeth at Jocelyn's indictment. "No, it's because I've seen you with Terrell and I have seen you with Jeff. Jeff is good for you and Terrell isn't. Can you honestly tell me you have forgotten all the things Terrell put you through?"

"No, I haven't forgotten. Those were growing pains and we put each other through things," Jocelyn retorted. "I don't want to talk about this anymore. My decision has been made. I choose Terrell."

Jocelyn finally got her mother off the phone. Her mother almost begged her to go back to Jeff and said she was going to get Jocelyn's father for telling her about Terrell. She told Jocelyn she wished she never gave Terrell her number and he stayed out of her life, and she would not allow Jocelyn to fall back into Terrell's trap before she hung up.

Jeff decided he wanted his ring back. He knew he was only doing it because he wanted to see Jocelyn and hoped she had changed her mind about the whole situation. Jeff called Jocelyn at work and was surprised when she picked up the phone. He was even more surprised at the disappointment which came over her voice when she realized it was him on the phone.

"Ouch," Jeff responded to her tone of voice.

"Ouch?" Jocelyn asked.

"I don't think I have ever been so rudely greeted in my life. I should be the one with the problem. Actually, I do have a problem. I want the ring back," Jeff told Jocelyn. He decided not to beat around the bush, and he no longer wanted to be the beacon of hope for a future between them.

Jocelyn hesitated and then said, "You can have it back. Where do you want to meet?"

"I'll come to your building at lunch, and you can come down and give it to me." Jeff told her.

"OK, see you at lunch time." Jocelyn began. "Jeff?" She called his name to catch him before he hung up.

"What?" Jeff answered.

"I'm sorry," Jocelyn admitted through her sniffles. She was starting to cry.

Jeff hung up the phone without responding. Jocelyn was really starting to rethink her decision. Everyone couldn't be wrong, she thought. What if things didn't work out between her and Terrell? Would she ever find anyone else like Jeff? She would talk to Jeff at lunch. She knew explaining was out of the question, but she could talk to him and get an idea about how he felt.

Chapter 16

At lunchtime, Jocelyn put on her coat and went downstairs to meet Jeff. She put the ring on her finger, wanting to see what Jeff would say about it being there. She stood outside for almost 15 minutes before Jeff showed up.

"I thought you weren't coming." Jocelyn spoke first.

"I almost didn't," Jeff admitted.

"Can we talk?" Jocelyn asked. "Do you have time now?"

"No. May I have the ring so I can return it and get my money back?" Jeff started. "Maybe the man will have mercy on me and take it back when he hears my story."

"Your story? Why are you saying it like I did something so bad to you? I told you I want to be sure, that's all," Jocelyn told him.

Jeff didn't say anything else to Jocelyn. He held out his hand for the ring and she stuck her hand out with the ring on it. Jeff didn't budge and didn't look Jocelyn directly in the face. Jocelyn saw her wearing the ring didn't have the intended effect, so she took it off and gave it to Jeff. She grabbed Jeff's hand when she put the ring into his hand. Jeff didn't move his hand or look at Jocelyn.

"I'm so sorry. You were nothing but great to me and I didn't mean to hurt you," Jocelyn said.

Jeff stood stiff as a board. He didn't want to be rude or come off cold, but he also didn't want to hear Jocelyn sit there and apologize.

"I have to go," Jeff told Jocelyn and pulled his hand and the ring back.

Jocelyn nodded her head to let Jeff know she understood. She looked at him for what could possibly be the last time and began to go back into the building. Jeff walked off and Jocelyn's heart dropped. She wondered how she could hurt a man like that. He was great to her. Damn Terrell and damn her feelings.

When Jocelyn returned to work, there were three messages from Karen on her voicemail. She didn't say why she wanted Jocelyn to call her, but Jocelyn knew it was because of Jeff. Jocelyn thought about it and decided she would call Karen when she got home. She had dedicated enough of her workday to explaining and dealing with the fall out of her decision. She wanted to try to get some work done. She thought about it and realized she should have taken another day off.

At home Jocelyn settled in and tried to call Terrell's cell phone again. He still didn't answer. She'd blocked her phone number, so how could he know it was her? She deliberated for a while and decided to call his mother's house. She prayed his mother didn't answer the phone. Not only did she answer the phone, but she began to tear into Jocelyn immediately after Jocelyn told her who she was.

"Why are you calling here?" Terrell's mother began. "Don't you think you have done enough damage? Why can't you leave well enough alone?"

Jocelyn attempted to explain, "I just need to talk to him. Please tell him I called."

"You have to be kidding me. No, I won't tell him. He's hurt right now but he would get over it if you would just stop calling him and talking to him," she told Jocelyn.

"I don't want to stop talking to him and I don't want him to get over it or me," Jocelyn admitted.

"Still a selfish bitch!" Terrell's mother yelled at Jocelyn. Jocelyn began to cry but Terrell's mother didn't stop. "So, what do you want him to do, wait for you, again? This isn't law school; you are getting married. Are you really that naive?"

"I'm not getting married," Jocelyn told her. "I broke the engagement off after Terrell came to see me the other night."

"What? You did what? Why?" Terrell's mother's voice changed.

"Because I realized I still love Terrell and I always will," Jocelyn told her through her sobs and sniffling.

Terrell's mother motioned to Terrell who'd just walked into the house from work. She told Jocelyn to hold on and told Terrell what Jocelyn just told her. Terrell shrugged and asked his mother why she was telling him. He said she of all people should know what Jocelyn was saying meant nothing and she could change her mind at the drop of a dime.

Terrell's mother came back to the phone and told her she tried to call Terrell, but he didn't pick up the phone. She suggested Jocelyn give Terrell time and not try to rush this because it is going to take Terrell time to get over the situation. She told Jocelyn she would talk to him when he got home but she wasn't making any promises.

Jocelyn thanked Mrs. Matthews and told her she was grateful for anything she could do. She reassured Mrs. Matthews she truly loved Terrell and would do anything necessary to make him believe it again. She hung up the phone and thought about it. Could she believe Mrs. Matthews would do anything to help her? History suggested she would rather see Jocelyn out of Terrell's life for good.

Jocelyn sat and debated her next move. What could she do to get to him? She had no intention of being patient. She had to let him know how she felt.

Jocelyn's phone began to ring. It was Karen again. Damn, Jocelyn thought, why is she sweating this so bad. She acts like I killed her mother or something. Jocelyn answered the phone with an attitude.

"Hello," Jocelyn said.

"Hi. Just tell me this is not true. Tell me Jeff is misunderstanding something. You broke off your engagement to him to be with Terrell?" Karen sped through her spiel.

"Yes, it is true." Jocelyn answered. "I really don't want to hear anyone's opinion on it."

"Are you kidding me? Because of Terrell you barely made it through law school. There are women all over this world looking for a good man like Jeff and you dump him for a not so good one?" Karen continued.

Jocelyn thought Karen must not have heard her say she wasn't opening the floor for comments, so she told her again. "I don't care what anyone thinks about my decision. I love him and we are going to be together."

"No, you're not. Jocelyn, you always get your hopes up about Terrell and it never happens. It's dependency or something. You were with Jeff and Terrell couldn't stand it. Now that you are not with Jeff, Terrell will forget all about you. You have been here before with him. He likes the fact he can get you to do things," Karen continued. She couldn't understand why Jocelyn couldn't remember all the things she went through with Terrell.

"It's different this time. It's going to work," Jocelyn told Karen.

Karen said in pure frustration, "Whatever girl. I will pray for you. I believe you are going to end up like you always do when you deal with Terrell. Hurt and alone."

Jocelyn said good-bye to Karen and told her not to call her again if she didn't have anything positive to say to her. She reminded Karen she didn't have a man and that possibly could be clouding her judgment. Karen sucked her teeth at Jocelyn. "Ignorance is definitely bliss," she added before she hung it up.

Jocelyn couldn't believe the nerve of Karen. It was none of her business anyway. 'She called me to chastise me for what I am doing. She should look at her own life', Jocelyn thought. 'She probably wants Jeff anyway. It was because of Karen that I noticed him. She was asking me if I thought he was handsome'.

Jocelyn went back to her thought process. What could she do to convince Terrell she is with him now and nothing else matters. She thought about the things Karen said and thought she was going to prove everyone wrong. She was sure that she had made the right decision. They would all see. Now if she could only convince Terrell.

Jocelyn got in her car and went to her parents' house. She wanted to talk to her father. He was the only one who understood her. She broke down as soon as she entered her parents' house. Her father came downstairs and saw his daughter laid out on the couch, crying and his heart dropped. He went to her and lifted her up to him.

"What's the matter baby?" Mr. McCrary asked.

"I may have made a big mistake," Jocelyn responded and began crying harder. "I broke off my engagement with Jeff. I decided I want to be with Terrell."

Mr. McCrary didn't know what to say. He just stared at his daughter. "Daddy, tell me I did the right thing," Jocelyn questioned and looked up at her father. Mr. McCrary hesitated. His wife usually handled this type of stuff. He had no idea whether Jocelyn made the right decision or not. He did, however, feel he'd done the right thing when he told Jocelyn what Terrell was there for. He finally got his bearings and began speaking, "How do you feel about your decision? Why did you come to your decision?"

"I love Terrell, Daddy," Jocelyn responded. Mr. McCrary was

looking for more than that, but her answer was enough for him.

Just as Mr. McCrary was about to speak again, Mrs. McCrary walked into the house. She looked at Jocelyn but kept walking. Mr. McCrary saw this and responded to his wife's silence. "You're not even going to acknowledge your daughter?"

"I see her," Mrs. McCrary responded, still walking away.

"Are you the reason she is upset?" he asked his wife.

"She is upset because she made the wrong decision and is feeling the effects of it," Mrs. McCrary answered from upstairs.

"That's not true. I have made the right decision. It's just not the decision you think is right!" Jocelyn yelled back. "You don't have to talk to me. I'll be fine."

"Then why are you here Joce?" Mrs. McCrary asked. "Why aren't you with Terrell celebrating your decision?"

That hit Jocelyn like a brick in the gut. How could her mother say something like that to her? The fact that she was right hurt the most. Jocelyn decided against telling them Terrell wasn't talking to her. She got up to leave but her father stopped her. He yelled his disapproval up to his wife. He didn't understand why his wife was acting the way she was toward Jocelyn, but it was going to stop right there.

"Honey, come down here!" Mr. McCrary hollered.

A couple of minutes passed, and Mrs. McCrary appeared. She looked at Jocelyn buried in her father's chest and smirked.

"Why is she crying? She should be happy," Mrs. McCrary was about to continue when Mr. McCrary waved his hand at her.

"What is wrong with you? How could you try to make the child go against her own heart?" he asked. "Why are you mad at her?"

"I'm mad at her because she accused me of only wanting her to be with Jeff because he is a lawyer and makes a lot of money," Mrs. McCrary answered. "I only want what's best for her as I always have, and I don't believe Terrell is it."

Mr. McCrary didn't know how to handle this. He didn't want to choose sides, but he was not going to have his wife not talking to their daughter. He knew he would have to approach this with kid gloves so as not to anger either of them.

"Joce, do you think your mom would ever tell you to marry someone for any other reason than love?" Mr. McCrary started.

Jocelyn shook her head no.

He continued, "Honey, have we ever had to question a decision Joce has made in the past?" His wife shook her head no. Mr. McCrary then looked at his wife and motioned her to come to him. He took his wife in his other arm and hugged them both close together.

"My beautiful women, I love you two," Mr. McCrary stated. "Don't ever put me through anything like this again. Are you two good?"

Chapter 17

Terrell had been dreading this moment more than any other moment in his life. He had to go see his son. That meant he had to deal with Lawanna's shit. He was not in the mood for her.

She started as soon as she opened the door. "Hey, hardheaded," Lawanna greeted Terrell.

"Not today, Lawanna," Terrell answered quickly. "Where is TJ?"

"Just answer one question. Why don't you ever get it? Do you like banging your head on a brick wall?" Lawanna didn't stop, "Why did you think it would be different this time?"

"Damn woman. Just get my son. I'm taking him for the weekend, right?" Terrell's voice boomed through the apartment.

"Don't be mad at me like I didn't tell you that Miss Thing would never be yours. She can't be. Her family won't allow it. You are not good enough for her in their eyes. So, even if she wanted you, her family would override it," Lawanna told Terrell before going upstairs to get TJ. Terrell sat on the couch and put his head in his hands. He began thinking Lawanna was right. Damn, he was stupid.

Jocelyn regained her composure and decided to leave. She just wanted to be alone with her thoughts. She knew that wouldn't happen in her parents' house. She took her father by the hand and led him out the door and to her car. When she looked up, she saw Terrell's car coming down the street. Before she could stop him, her father rushed toward the car. He was ordering Terrell to get out of the car, but Terrell didn't budge.

"Get out the car," Mr. McCrary said to Terrell.

Terrell then began to point to the back seat, alerting him to the child in the back seat. Jocelyn saw this and screamed out to her father. "Let him go!"

Her father looked back at her, and she nodded her head. Mr. McCrary stared Terrell down before moving out of the way of the car. Terrell didn't drive off right away. He was too shocked and needed time to breathe. He looked at Jocelyn and then at her father who was still staring him down as he walked away.

Jocelyn's next thought was to go try to talk to Terrell herself. She decided against it and just waved at him. He didn't wave back. He gave her one more look before he sped off down the street. Jocelyn went up to her father and gave him a big hug. She thanked him for caring.

"Give him time," Jocelyn said. She surprised herself as much as she surprised her father. "He did watch me get engaged to someone else."

"I know, but I hate to see you hurt. I just want to do something," He answered. He was still holding his daughter tight.

Jocelyn broke free for her father's clutch. She had to go. She had to be alone to plan her next move. She got in her car and as she drove off, she saw her father still watching her. She thought about all the trouble she was causing and how sad she was making the men in her life.

She didn't feel like going home but she didn't know where else to go. There was no one to turn to. Nobody understood what she was going through. She decided to go out for a drink. She stopped at the first bar she saw. She had never been to that bar before and wondered why.

When she stepped inside, it became clear why. Apparently, it was clear to everyone else in the bar too because they were staring at her. Jocelyn didn't care. She went straight up to the bar. The bartender finally came over and Jocelyn ordered a shot of Hennessy. That was just what the guy a couple of stools over needed to stir up a conversation.

"That is a lot of drink for a woman like you," he said and smiled at her. Jocelyn looked at him but didn't say anything. When the bartender put the shot down, she threw it back like she had seen people do so many times before. It was burning her throat and chest. The bartender and the man both started laughing. Jocelyn still didn't respond to them. Instead, she ordered another one.

"Whoa! Slow down lady," The guy spoke again. Still Jocelyn didn't respond.

The bartender on the other hand did. "Leave her alone."

"Man, I ain't bothering her but something is," The man answered. "And you and I both know letting her get drunk is not going to solve it."

"She ain't drunk but there is something bothering her," The bartender agreed. "What's wrong lady?"

Jocelyn finally responded to the two men. "Nothing but you ain't serving me drinks as fast as you should be." The bartender responded to that by setting a double shot in front of Jocelyn.

The bartender stared at Jocelyn for a minute. He didn't appreciate her attitude and was about to tell her about it when someone walked up and told him to chill. Jocelyn turned around when she heard the voice. It sounded familiar but she couldn't place it. She was shocked to see Michael standing over her.

"What are you doing Jocelyn?" Mike asked.

"Drinking. Damn why is that a problem for everyone here? Do I need to go to another bar?"

"Jocelyn, why are you drinking?" Mike asked. He started feeling like the bartender but didn't act on it. "What is wrong?"

"I messed up. OK? Is that what you want to hear? Is that what everyone needs to hear? I messed up!" Jocelyn screamed. Everyone in the bar turned to look at her. She burst into tears and fell into Mike's arms. Mike didn't quite know what to do then.

"Come over here and talk to me," he said.

"Why?" Jocelyn asked. "Why would I talk to you?"

"OK, I see you are an even nastier drunk than you are a person," Mike told her.

"You don't even know me. You never tried to know me. Just talked shit about me," Jocelyn answered. She was slurring her words, and this made her laugh out loud. She had never been drunk before but had heard stories from other people about being drunk.

"I know you were my girlfriend's best friend but never talked to me when you saw me," he shot back at her. "I know you walked around high school with your nose turned up and now I see you here drunk because what? Your lawyer boyfriend dumped you?"

"That is not why I am here. He didn't dump me. I am here because I dumped him for your boy, and I messed up," she told him.

"My boy? Terrell? Are you still messing around with that?" Mike asked. "He was never really my boy."

"Whatever. Now neither one of them will talk to me," Jocelyn said, still slurring. "What can I do to get Terrell back?"

"You want him back instead of the lawyer?" Mike couldn't believe his ears. "Why?"

"I love him," Jocelyn answered.

"Whoa. Didn't expect that to come out of your mouth," Mike

started. "When did you figure this out?"

"I've always known that." She gave Mike a suspicious look. "Why?"

Mike looked at Jocelyn for a minute. "No reason. Just asking."

"No, you're not. What did he tell you?" Jocelyn asked.

"Nothing recently. I haven't spoken to him in years," Mike answered. "He never thought you loved him."

Jocelyn looked at Mike like he had three heads. At this point he kind of did. She couldn't believe Terrell didn't think she loved him. She was thinking to herself what would she have to do to prove to him how she felt? She thought that she did a good job showing and telling him when they were together. She couldn't believe this. She attempted to get up and run out, but Henny had another plan. She staggered and fell back toward the table.

"I know you didn't think you were going to drive. Where do you live?" Mike asked her.

"I tripped. I'm good," Jocelyn answered. "I don't need your commentary."

"You don't need to drive either and I am not going to let you," he responded. "Whatever differences we had in the past don't matter. I wouldn't let you drive in your condition."

"My condition?" she questioned.

Then she attempted to leave again. She got to the door and Mike was there blocking it. He shook his head and picked Jocelyn up by the waist and carried her out of the place. She tried to break free but couldn't. She recognized her car and pointed it out to Mike.

Mike kept going until he got to his car. He blocked her in with his leg and opened the door. He shoved her in, locking the door behind her. He ran around to the driver's side, looking back to make sure she didn't try to get out. She didn't. When he got in the car, he was a little afraid because she was sitting still, not moving at all. He called her name a couple times before she answered. He asked her again where she lived, and she didn't answer.

Mike had no idea where she lived and thought about taking her to Monique's house. The more he thought about it, the worse that idea felt. He didn't want to deal with her. She would probably accuse him of sleeping with her. Dang, he thought, he didn't remember where her parents lived either. He wouldn't do that to her. He couldn't imagine her parents would understand him dropping their drunken daughter off.

Chapter 18

Jocelyn woke up the next morning with no idea of where she was. The place looked a little familiar, but she was still groggy and couldn't think. She tried to recall the night before and remembered Mike. She called out his name, but he didn't answer. She then checked her clothes. She didn't have any on. What the hell happened? Why would he do that to her? She thought maybe she shouldn't assume he did anything to her.

She got up and walked around the room looking for her clothes. She found them in a chair. They were neatly folded and smelled like they had been washed. This made her more worried about what happened the night before. She couldn't believe he had the nerve to wash her clothes. Jocelyn began putting the clothes on and was heading toward the door when she bumped right into him. Only, it wasn't Mike. It was Terrell.

"Why are you here? Did Mike call you?" Jocelyn asked.

"I'm here because I live here. What are you doing here? What were you doing drinking shots of Henny in a bar?" he asked. The look on his face said it all. He really didn't feel like being polite to Jocelyn.

"I went out for a drink or two. Why is everyone making a big deal about this? How did I get here?"

"No. It's no big deal. That is why you don't know how you got here. What were you thinking?" He asked. "What if Mike wouldn't have been there?"

"I would have been fine. You didn't answer my question. How did I get here?" she asked.

Terrell looked at Jocelyn for a minute. He shook his head thinking about what Mike told him when he dropped her off. He watched her as she continued to get dressed and then it hit him.

"Where did you think you were Jocelyn?" Terrell asked.

"I didn't know where I was or how I got here. That is why I am asking. All I remember is Mike, so I assumed I was at his house," she said, wondering what he was implying.

"Jocelyn," Terrell started but decided against what he was going to say.

Jocelyn looked when he called her name. She was waiting for him to continue but he didn't. "What?" Jocelyn asked.

"Nothing. I was just wondering if you needed a ride to your car," He replied.

"Yes, thank you." She forgot she didn't have her car. "Terrell, thank you."

"For what?" he asked.

"For making sure I was ok. For not telling Mike to take me somewhere else, anywhere else but here," she said and smiled at him.

"I wouldn't do that, and Mike wasn't taking you anywhere else after you threw up in his car," Terrell answered laughing. "He was mad about that."

Jocelyn started laughing with him. She didn't remember throwing up in the car. She didn't even remember getting in the car. Jocelyn reached out and hugged Terrell. He stood stiff.

"I know you need time to trust me again or to even think about dealing with me. I just want you to know that I do love you and I am sorry you had to go through the whole thing with Jeff."

Terrell loosened up a little and turned to look Jocelyn in her face.

He still didn't hug her back or move too much. Jocelyn realized she was still hugging him, so she let him go and touched his face. He didn't respond to that either. Jocelyn continued to look at him, smiling.

"Well, we better get you to your car before someone steals it in that neighborhood," he said as he moved away from Jocelyn. She nodded in agreement.

Jocelyn felt relief when she got in her car. She knew Terrell would come around now. She just had to figure out how to get him there. She attempted to remember what happened last night. She also thought about throwing up in Mike's car. She would have to get his information from Terrell and pay for the car to be cleaned out. She couldn't help laughing at the thought of Mike rushing her to Terrell's after she threw up.

Her head was pounding. She vowed never to drink again. How the hell did she get here, was all she could think. She must have looked so pathetic when she was dropped off at Terrell's house. As her mind continued to spin, she wondered why Mike had taken her there. There were other places he could have taken her to, so why did he take her to Terrell's and what was said during the exchange?

At home, Jocelyn only had one thing on her mind—sleep. She looked at her phone and saw there were four messages. They would have to wait until later. As she climbed the stairs to her bedroom the phone rang again. 'Dang, I forgot to turn the ringer off', she thought. She crawled back down to turn the ringer off. When she woke up Terrell had left her a voicemail. He was calling to make sure she got home ok. She thought about calling him back but didn't know what she would say to him at that moment, so she just turned the phone off and crawled upstairs.

Chapter 19

When Jocelyn woke up to the same pain in her head. She went downstairs to get some aspirin and decided to check her messages. The first message was from her mother telling her to call. So was the second message. The third message was from Monique and the fourth was from Jeff. A thousand questions were going through her head. Why he would be calling her was the most pressing.

Curiosity got the best of her, so she returned Jeff's call first.

"Hello Jeff," Jocelyn said, not knowing what she was going to get.

"Hey. Hi. How are you doing?" Jeff answered. He was almost overly chipper, but Jocelyn thought nothing of it.

"So?" Jocelyn replied. "What can I help you with?"

"What do you mean?" Jeff answered. "Didn't you want me to call you?"

"Where would you get that idea?" Jocelyn asked.

"Your mother. She called me and said you realized the mistake you made, and you have changed your mind about Terrell," he said, the enthusiasm was leaving his voice.

Jocelyn felt like she could murder her mother. She was so mad her head was about to explode or was that just from the hangover? "I never said that. I am so sorry she did that to you."

"Yeah. Why would I think you would come to your senses? You obviously lost your mind a long time ago," Jeff responded.

"Excuse me? I said I am sorry for my mother. What else do you want?" Jocelyn demanded.

"Nothing. Absolutely nothing but for you and your mother to stay away from me."

Jeff's hostility was over the top in Jocelyn's mind but all she did was say, "Done."

Jeff hung up the phone before Jocelyn could say anything else. Not that she had anything else to say to him. She couldn't believe her mother would do that. It was a whole different level of cruelty. What was she thinking?

"Mama, how could you?" Jocelyn screamed as soon as her mother answered the phone. "Didn't you think Jeff was in enough pain?"

"The only person I saw hurt was you." Her mother answered. "I just didn't want to let Jeff get away. I am surprised he was as receptive as he was. Don't let him get away."

"Well, he is not receptive anymore. I didn't know why he was calling me, so I asked him why he was calling, and he didn't take it well. Apparently, I was supposed to know that my mother is psychotic and would tell the man I want him back when I said no such thing."

"Don't get smart with me," Her mother snapped.

"Mom, just explain what made you do that?" Jocelyn pleaded.

"I just don't want to see you waste your life away waiting for a man who will never be ready or worthy." Her mother's answer cut like a knife. Why would she think Terrell is not worthy?

"What are you talking about? Terrell was obviously ready because he came over to ask Dad if he could marry me! Why can't you leave well enough alone? I can make my own decisions!" Jocelyn yelled at her mother. Her mother wasn't pleased with Jocelyn and let her know it by slamming the phone down in her ear.

Jocelyn just shook her head. She couldn't believe the nerve of her mother. What could make a person do something like that? She thought about Jeff and what he must be thinking about her right now. She tried to think of what she thought of herself right now. Was she choosing Terrell because he was familiar? How do you know you love someone you haven't been with in years? Sure they talked, but why would that make her think they were still in love?

She thought deeper. If Terrell thought she never loved him, why would he think she would marry him? Why would she marry him? What had changed between them to make them think they could make a marriage work when they couldn't make their relationship work before? Now she was wondering if she actually had made a mistake.

Jocelyn picked up the phone and called the only person who could answer her questions.

"Why did you want to marry me?" Jocelyn asked immediately when Terrell answered the phone.

"I love you," he answered.

"Why? Why after all the time we spent apart do you love me?" she asked.

"I just do. I never stopped loving you. Do you love me?" he responded.

"I feel like I do? I don't understand it though." Jocelyn's answer was more a question than an answer.

"Gee thanks." Terrell laughed at her response.

"I don't mean it like that. I know why I love you. I just don't understand how we got here," she started. "We spent the last ten years apart, most of it with no contact. I thought about you over the years."

"I know but I felt it the moment I saw you in the mall," he told her.

"Really?" she asked.

"I knew something was missing in my life and it felt like I found the answer when I saw you." Terrell's words floored Jocelyn, but she wasn't ready to concede just yet.

"Can we make it work?" she asked. "We weren't able to make it work in the past. I want to be married for the rest of my life to one person."

"So do I," Terrell answered quickly. "I know we can make it work because we are friends also."

"I'm sorry," Jocelyn responded.

"Sorry about what?" he asked.

"About everything. I never meant to hurt you. I didn't mean to hurt anyone. Now Jeff thinks I am a bad person, and my mother is not speaking to me. I have made a mess of everything," Jocelyn said. "I love you."

"Your mother is mad at you because of me?" He asked. He thought about what people had always told him about her parents not accepting him. Dang they were right. He couldn't believe this.

Jocelyn's answer shocked him. "No. She is mad at me because I yelled at her. She told Jeff I changed my mind and wanted him back."

"What? Is that true?" Terrell asked before he could even filter it.

"No. That is why I yelled at her. I couldn't understand why she would do something like that," Jocelyn said. Thinking about the whole situation made her sad.

Terrell said, "I know why she would do it. I am not good enough for you in her eyes, but Jeff is."

"That isn't true. She just thought about our history and didn't think we are right for each other because of our past," Jocelyn answered in a hurry.

"Yeah. OK." Jocelyn could hear the change in Terrell's voice.

Jocelyn's voice broke Terrell's thought. She was asking him where they went from here. He thought about it but didn't have a ready response. He didn't know if he was ready to get caught up with her again just yet. She asked to come see him to talk and after a brief pause, he agreed to it.

When they hung up Terrell began having second thoughts. He really wasn't ready and the fact that her mother had a problem with them being together made him even more nervous about putting himself out there. What if she decided to listen to her mother? Damn. Why did he have to fall in love with her? He thought about it more and decided he wouldn't call her back and cancel but hoped she wouldn't let him down.

Chapter 20

Jocelyn and Terrell had been back together for a couple of months and he still hadn't proposed to her. She really thought he would have. They'd spent almost every waking moment together if they weren't working. They even met up for lunch sometimes. They talked a lot, checking in with each other, making sure they were on the same page. They didn't do that when they were younger. Things were going great, in her mind. She was starting to think about all the things people told her, that he only wanted her because she was with someone else. She could feel her friends and family looking at them, waiting for them to announce their engagement. They were probably having a field day talking about them behind their backs, she thought.

A flurry of other thoughts went through her mind. Why hadn't he proposed? What if he never proposed? Could she live with not getting married? Had she done something to make him not propose? She searched her memory to see if she could find something but found nothing.

She knew better than to talk to anyone about it because she would only get "I told you so" and sideways stares that implied that "she let that good man get away." Even if they didn't say it, she knew it would be there lingering. What could she do? Talk to him? She didn't want to rush him or find out he didn't want it. She would just have to suck it up and talk to him about it.

The phone snapped her out of her thoughts. It was Monique. Dang. She answered it but really didn't feel like talking to her. She tried to think of a reason to get off the phone with Monique but couldn't. Then Monique dropped a bombshell on her.

"When is your wedding? I only ask so I will know if I can attend since I am not going to be part of your wedding party."

"We haven't set a date yet. Why are you saying you are not going to be in my wedding party? You don't want to be part of my wedding party?" Jocelyn turned it around on Monique.

"No, I am not saying that. I just thought I would know things first, being one of your oldest friends," she answered.

Jocelyn rolled her eyes. This is precisely why she didn't want to talk to Monique. "You will be. There is nothing to tell. The truth is he hasn't even proposed yet."

Jocelyn regretted telling her that. Why did she say that? She definitely didn't want to say that to Monique. She awaited Monique's barrage but all she got was "Oh!". That "oh" held a lot of weight but Jocelyn wasn't in the mood to question it. She had enough fears and anxieties about the situation without Monique's commentary, so she attempted to change the subject. She asked Monique what was going on with her and if she was seeing anyone. Not much and no were Monique's short but not so sweet answers.

Jocelyn was still trying to figure out how to get Monique off the phone. She didn't want to sound rude, but she didn't want to talk about it. Monique let Jocelyn off the hook. She told her that she only called to ask when the wedding was and didn't mean to hold her up. Jocelyn was relieved but also saddened by the fact Monique had only called her for that. They used to be so close and could talk about anything. Jocelyn tried to think back to when the tide changed. She was about to ask Monique if they could hang out some time when she realized Monique was no longer on the phone.

The conversation with Monique and the way it ended stayed on Jocelyn's mind for the rest of the day and into the night. She was sitting on the couch with Terrell, and he asked her what was bothering her.

"Monique and I used to be so close. I am trying to figure out what happened," Jocelyn answered. That was the immediate thing on her mind, but she was also still wondering about them. Her mind was spinning overtime.

"I know sometimes people grow apart. It is a part of life. I hadn't thought you were that close anymore for a long time. Why are you so concerned about it now?" Terrell asked nonchalantly.

"I guess I was so busy I didn't notice our friendship slipping away. Wow. How could I not notice?" Jocelyn was not letting it go that easily.

"It's called life. Sometimes it happens. Especially when two people are going in different directions," he answered.

Jocelyn smiled at him. She wasn't completely satisfied with the answer, but she let him know she appreciated him listening.

"Terrell," Jocelyn called his name.

"Yes," he answered and looked at her, sensing something was wrong from the way she called his name.

"Will you marry me?" Jocelyn asked. She shocked herself and the look on Terrell's face showed he was shocked as well.

He just stared at Jocelyn then a smile came across his face. "Of course, I will." He turned back and started watching TV.

"No, I don't think you understand." Jocelyn got up from Terrell's arms and turned to face him. "I have loved you since the day I met you. I know I have messed up in the past, but I am sincere and I want you in my life for the rest of our lives."

Terrell didn't know what to say to Jocelyn's confession. He took her back in his arms and held her. "I love you too. I've loved you since the day we met." Then he got up and walked away. Jocelyn was so confused at this point. She had just poured her heart out to this man, and he got up and walked away. 'Oh my God,' Jocelyn thought, 'everyone is right. He never had any intention of marrying me. He just wanted me because someone else had me. How could I be so stupid?'"

Just as she finished her thought Terrell walked back into the room. Jocelyn thought about telling him exactly how she felt at the moment, but she looked at him and felt something come over her.

"To do this right," Terrell announced. "We need this." He opened a box and showed Jocelyn a ring. Jocelyn was overwhelmed. Terrell then got down on one knee. "My impatient lady, will you do me the honor of being my wife?" Jocelyn grabbed Terrell by his head, nodding hers up and down. "I can't hear you," Terrell said laughing.

"Yes. Yes. Yes." Jocelyn was crying now. She looked at him, smiling through her tears.

Terrell held her and attempted to put the ring on, but Jocelyn was shaking so bad he handed it to her. She looked at it and kissed him before she put the ring on her finger and stuck it out for both of them to admire. Terrell was smiling. He never thought he would see this day. He was trying to find the right moment while accruing the nerve to ask Jocelyn to marry him. He grabbed Jocelyn tighter to him and thought he never wanted to let her go. 'God don't let her change her mind,' he thought.

"Who should we call first?" Jocelyn finally spoke.

"Can we just enjoy it tonight and make all the calls in the morning?" He was still giving her time to let it marinate in her mind.

"Yeah," Jocelyn answered. She was kind of puzzled by his answer, but she was so happy. Relieved was a better word but happy, nonetheless.

Jocelyn and Terrell spent the rest of the night the same way it started, sitting on his couch in each other's arms. They continued watching the movie they were watching and occasionally they gave each other a look. They fell asleep right there on the couch.

Chapter 21

The next morning Terrell awoke first. He stared down at Jocelyn and still couldn't believe that she had agreed to marry him. He thought about going upstairs to tell his mother but decided to wait for Jocelyn. He was still staring when Jocelyn woke up.

"What's wrong?" Jocelyn asked when she saw Terrell watching her.

"Nothing. Just admiring my future wife, wondering how I got so lucky," Terrell answered. "You still want to be my wife, right?"

"Of course, I do. Why would you ask me that?" Jocelyn asked.

"I'm just thinking about what happened to the last brother." Terrell laughed like he was joking but he was dead serious. "I don't want to end up like him."

"Terrell, that is not funny. I didn't mean to hurt him," Jocelyn shot back at Terrell. He apologized and asked her if she wanted to go out for breakfast and then tell her parents. Jocelyn agreed and they proceeded to the shower to start their first day as an engaged couple.

After breakfast they went to Jocelyn's parents' house. They both sat in the car, not moving. Terrell finally looked over at Jocelyn and asked if they were going in. She nodded and told him that she was just thinking about all the events which led to this moment and how her parents were really going to react now that it was a reality. This made Terrell nervous. He thought about what Lawanna told him: her parents would never let her marry him. He must have tensed up because Jocelyn asked him what was wrong.

"Nervous. That's all. Never been here before," Terrell answered.

"It'll be fine. They know you. They know us. It'll be good." Jocelyn wasn't sure but she tried to assure Terrell.

As soon as they got into the house Jocelyn stuck the ring in her mother's face. Her mother looked impressed. She examined it for a couple of seconds and looked up at Terrell and congratulated him. She then turned to her daughter, hugged her, and said the same.

"I just wish your father was home to enjoy this moment," she told them. "He went out to lunch with some buddies. He should be back soon if you want to wait."

Jocelyn looked at Terrell who was just standing there smiling. Jocelyn really didn't want to tell anyone else before she told her father, but if Terrell had other plans they could come back.

"Do you want to wait for my father?" Jocelyn broke him out of his thoughts.

"We can. I'm going to see my son and let you ladies talk. Call me when he gets home," Terrell told her.

She went to him, kissed him, and hugged him tight.

"What's that for?" he asked.

"There's going to be a whole lot of that for the rest of our lives for no reason at all. Have fun with your son," Jocelyn answered before letting him go.

Terrell thought about how he would tell his son he was getting married. He knew if he told TJ, he would have to tell Lawanna and he did not feel like hearing her mouth. He thought about it again and thought 'Oh well, no time like the present', and not even Lawanna could bring him down at this moment. He got to the house and took a deep breath before he went in.

"Why are you grinning from ear to ear?" Lawanna asked as soon as she saw Terrell.

"Funny you should ask. I got engaged last night," he answered.

"To who?" She shot back. The look on her face bordered on rage.

"What do you mean 'to who'? You know who," Terrell answered.

"Hmmm. Have you told her parents yet?" Lawanna asked with a smirk. Her victory was short lived because Terrell answered that they just told her mother, and she gave her blessing.

"Well, I don't want her around my son." Lawanna dropped the bomb. Terrell thought nothing could bring him down. He was wrong. That did it.

"What? What the hell do you mean you don't want her around your son? He is my son too and she is my fiancée. They are going to be spending a lot of time together!" Terrell yelled.

"Naw! No, they ain't. If I find out she was anywhere near my son, I will make sure you don't see him," Lawanna threatened.

"Try me woman and you will never see him again. Who do you think the courts will believe is more fit to raise him, a woman who has men running through her house on a regular basis or a stable, working, married couple? You better learn to think before you speak," Terrell countered.

"She ain't going to be around my son and that is final, Terrell," Lawanna answered.

Terrell was just curious at this point. He already knew what he had to do but he wanted to know why Lawanna didn't like Jocelyn. "What is your beef with Jocelyn? She didn't do anything to you. I thought you were friends in high school?"

"She isn't anyone's friend. Just ask Monique. She doesn't know how to be a friend. One day she likes you, the next she doesn't, and I don't want her to get my son like that," Lawanna answered.

"That's bullshit and you know it. I don't know what happened between you and Jocelyn but don't use Monique as an example. They are just going in different directions. They are still friends."

"Terrell. You believe what you want to believe about your 'princess'. You probably don't even want her, just the thought of obtaining what you could never fully have. That is what I've heard. That you like the challenge, the chase. What are you going to do now that you have caught her?"

Terrell was floored by Lawanna's comment. That is what she heard? Where did she hear that from? He decided not to feed into Lawanna's trap. Who would possibly say something like that? "You know what I'm going to do? Marry her. I don't know who came up with those conspiracy theories, but I am very much in love and ready to settle down," Terrell answered after gaining his composure.

"Where is my son?" Terrell thought it was funny that TJ didn't come running after hearing his voice.

"He is at my mother's house. Why?" Lawanna answered with a smirk.

"You know I didn't come here to see you. Why didn't you just tell me that he wasn't here? What? You got a rendezvous planned?"

"Forget you, Terrell. Don't try to act all high and mighty and make me feel like dirt for living my life!" she shouted at Terrell.

"Oh yeah, whoever he is, don't have that dude around my son," Terrell said with a laugh but an air of seriousness that made Lawanna do a double take. "As a matter of fact, don't have any of them lame dudes you be messing with around my son." At that Terrell stormed out of

Lawanna's apartment.

Terrell began thinking about his next step as he walked back to Jocelyn's parents' house. How does he let Lawanna get to him every time?

Terrell got back to Jocelyn's parents' house and pretended the conversation with Lawanna never happened. Jocelyn could tell there was something wrong, but she didn't push it when Terrell said he was just upset because his son wasn't there. He was happy to see that Jocelyn and her mom were making out the guest list for the wedding as well as discussing other wedding-related things. He sat beside Jocelyn and began thinking about his guest list. He didn't have many people he wanted to invite, probably just his family.

As if Jocelyn was reading his mind she asked, "what is the total number of people you want to come to the wedding?"

"That is up to you and your mother. I will be happy with just us and the minister, but it is your day so whatever you choose is fine," he answered softly.

Jocelyn smiled at him but still couldn't shake the feeling that something was wrong with him. She slowly turned her attention back to her mother and the planning they were doing.

When Jocelyn's father came home Jocelyn rushed him, jumping in his arms. Her dad didn't know what he did to deserve this, but it felt good. It had been a long time since he had seen his baby girl this happy. He looked across the room and saw Terrell sitting there and then it hit him why she was so happy. Jocelyn bounced off her father and showed him the engagement ring. He smiled and tried not to show the worry that he felt. It didn't work.

"Daddy what's wrong? Jocelyn asked.

He tried to joke it away. "I thought you were hugging me like that because of something I did."

"Oh! Daddy I am. You are the one that told me that Terrell wanted to be with me," Jocelyn responded.

He thought to himself, 'Gee don't remind me.'

At the time he thought it was a good idea and that his daughter should have the opportunity to choose who she wanted to be with, but now he wasn't so sure if Terrell was the person he wanted to entrust his daughter's future to. He knew it was Jocelyn's decision, but wished there was something someone could say to her that wouldn't sound anti-Terrell before she walked down the aisle.

Jocelyn was still looking at her father. She knew there was something wrong with him. This worried her but she didn't want to think of it being the obvious. Why would he tell her that Terrell wanted to be with her if he didn't want her to be with Terrell? Jocelyn thought she would give it one more try before she moved on. "Daddy you still look so sad. Are you sure there is nothing wrong?"

"Nothing but an old sentimental fool losing his little girl. I'll be fine," he stated.

He then went over to where Terrell sat and extended his hand. "Are you sure this is what you want and that you can take care of my little girl?"

Terrell just looked at Jocelyn and then at her father and said, "This is what I have wanted since the day I met her. I knew we weren't ready then, but we are ready now." Terrell then got up and shook Mr. McCrary's hand, a strong, firm shake, thinking that would be of some reassurance to him.

For the rest of the afternoon, Jocelyn, and her mother continued planning and Terrell and Jocelyn's dad sat and watched sports. Terrell thought it felt right. He had always thought of Jocelyn's family as his family, even when they weren't together, but this felt different. It felt like this was the way it should be. It put a big smile on his face. Damn what Lawanna and everyone else thought. This was it for him.

On the way home, Jocelyn joked that she thought her mother had the whole wedding all planned out. She was laughing but Terrell wasn't, so she asked him what was wrong. Nothing was his answer. "I'm just listening to you," he continued.

"If there is something wrong, please tell me," Jocelyn responded. She could even hear the difference in his voice. "Are you happy?"

"Very. This is the happiest I have been in my life," he responded. It really was, but he couldn't shake the feeling that something was going to go wrong.

"Really? There is nothing bothering you?" Jocelyn asked again.

Terrell shook his head and looked straight out at the road. Jocelyn went back to the things her, and her mother discussed about the wedding even though she felt Terrell wasn't listening. She thought she would make sure he wasn't. "Honey, you have to make a list of the people you want to attend the wedding."

"My mom can do that. There is no one in particular I want to come except my son, so I'll leave it up to her," he answered.

Jocelyn was totally surprised. She thought for sure he wasn't listening. "OK" was all she could say.

When they got home it was more of the same from Terrell. He was definitely being distant. Jocelyn just decided to ignore it, figuring that if he wanted to talk about it, he would say something. They ate dinner in silence and then Jocelyn thought of something else.

"Who are going to be your groomsmen?" she asked.

Terrell hadn't even thought about that and was honest about it. "How many do I need? I don't have as many friends as I used to.

"I don't know either. I think I will have a maid of honor and one bridesmaid. Does that sound good?" Jocelyn thought about it and realized she didn't have as many friends as she used to either.

"Yeah. That's fine," Terrell answered. "So that's settled. Who do you want to be your maid of honor?"

"I was thinking of asking Monique," Jocelyn answered. "She freaked out before when she thought I didn't include her."

Terrell's mind went back to the conversation he had with Lawanna about Jocelyn and Monique's friendship and wondered if he should mention it to Jocelyn. His mouth opened to say something, but he couldn't find the words to tell his fiancée that it may not be a good idea to include Monique, so he just nodded at Jocelyn's decision.

"What do you want to do tonight?" Jocelyn asked. "I'm in the mood for a movie."

"Yeah. We can do that," Terrell responded.

He wasn't really in the mood, but he didn't want Jocelyn to keep asking him what was wrong so he'd to just go along with the flow. They both went into their own thoughts at that moment. Little did they know they were thinking the same thing: that they were actually getting married.

Jocelyn said it first, "We're really getting married?"

Terrell's eyes opened wide. "What? Why are you asking that?"

"It's not a question, it's an observation," Jocelyn responded. "You have to admit, we didn't take the most conventional road to this point." Jocelyn smiled at the end of that statement, mostly to calm Terrell's nerves.

Terrell smiled back at Jocelyn, "Yeah. I guess not but all of that doesn't matter now, does it?"

"Not at all," Jocelyn told him. She got up from where she sat, went to him, and gave him a small kiss on his forehead followed by another on his lips. At this point Terrell felt everything would be fine.

Chapter 22

Jocelyn woke to reality. She and Terrell were engaged. They were getting married. She looked up to the sky and thought to herself that she never thought they would get to this point. She then turned and watched Terrell sleep. Forever she thought. Forever. She has loved this man forever.

Terrell began to move so Jocelyn closed her eyes and pretended to be asleep. Terrell wasn't buying that Jocelyn was asleep for some reason. He kissed her on her forehead, then her lips. He then pulled the sheets off her and roamed lower. Jocelyn didn't give up the charade. She kept her eyes closed but moaned at every touch.

When Terrell reached her navel Jocelyn jumped up. She couldn't take it anymore.

"Good morning my fiancée," Terrell said and continued to circle her navel with his tongue.

In between gasps Jocelyn managed to say good morning in return. She was thinking how good it was to hear the word fiancée. That thought was replaced when Terrell dove lower. He didn't even bother to take off her PJs. She thought she could definitely wake up like this every day.

Terrell must have read her mind because that is exactly what he asked her. "How would you like to wake up to that for the rest of your life. The rest of our life. Sounds good to me," Terrell added and went back to what he was doing. Jocelyn was nodding but she couldn't talk anymore. Yeah, it definitely sounded good to her.

Jocelyn showered and made breakfast. While doing that, she realized they had forgotten the most important thing—the date. Jocelyn knew that once she started telling people about their engagement, that would be the first question they asked. 'When are they getting married?' She would ask Terrell as soon as he came downstairs.

Terrell immediately noticed the troubled look on Jocelyn's face when he came down to get breakfast. He wondered if this was it if Jocelyn had changed her mind. All his insecurities came to the surface, and he wanted to just bolt or tell her to forget the whole thing. Damn, everyone was right.

Jocelyn broke his train of thought. "Honey, when are we going to get married."

"Huh?" Terrell asked. He was totally thrown for a loop. "Oh, whenever you want to."

"We need a date. You know that is what everyone is going to ask," Jocelyn responded. "We need to have a date to give them."

"I know, but I don't have one in mind. I thought we should tell them we are engaged then get together and figure out the best time for us to get married. I'm new at this so correct me if I am wrong," Terrell answered. He really hoped he was right because he had no idea when a good time was to get married.

"Yeah, you are right. I am just so nervous about telling everyone. I thought my parents would be the hardest, but I don't know," Jocelyn said.

"What's so hard about it?" Terrell asked. He was really curious to hear her answer.

"It's hard because people haven't always been supportive of our relationship," Jocelyn answered.

"Well, those aren't the people I want at the wedding anyway. If they can't be happy for us, then they can do it somewhere other than our wedding. I don't care if it is just me and you because in the end that is all that matters: me and you." Jocelyn could hear the irritation in his voice, so she decided to change the subject. Sort of.

"So, what time of year would you like to get married?" Jocelyn asked.

"Anytime you want to. Just tell me the time, place, and what color my tux has to be, and I will be there with bells on," Terrell answered with a laugh. Jocelyn gave him a puzzled look. He caught on and continued. "Weddings are usually the woman's brainchild. Men aren't usually that involved in the planning." He hoped the look on Jocelyn's face would go away but it didn't. "So, what time of year do you want to get married, Jocelyn?" Terrell asked. She smiled and it was like a weight lifted off.

"I always wanted a winter wedding," Jocelyn answered.

"OK. Winter is as good a time as any," Terrell answered.

"No, I want a winter themed wedding," Jocelyn stated. "I think it is so beautiful in the winter. The snow is glistening, lights shining off of it." She looked over at Terrell for his reaction and he looked like he was picturing it.

"What if it doesn't snow on our wedding day?" he asked.

"That is why we make the snow or the appearance of the snow. I am not crazy. I would not get married outside in the winter," Jocelyn said and shot Terrell a look.

"I know you are not crazy. I'm just trying to catch up and see what you see. It sounds beautiful," Terrell answered. He walked over to Jocelyn and kissed her. "Is this something we will be able to do or will a professional need to do it?"

"I don't know but I can look into it," Jocelyn answered. She wondered if he was really on board or was this part of his 'anytime, anywhere and I will be there with bells on' theory.

"What else do you see, baby?" Terrell asked. This threw Jocelyn off. She guessed she was wrong about the disinterest on Terrell's part.

"I want it to be a sit-down dinner wedding. With tables and centerpieces of winter lilies. A total white winter wonderland." Jocelyn continued. She could actually see it. She turned to him and looked him up and down. "I want you and the groomsmen in black though. I think black tuxes look better than white ones, they are more classic. You can wear ivory or snow-white cummerbunds and ties."

Terrell was totally into what Jocelyn was saying. He never thought about what his wedding would look like other than having him in it; and in several of his thoughts, Jocelyn was there too. The reality was sounding a whole lot better than the dream. "OK, so what is the date?"

Jocelyn gave him a look. She couldn't believe how well this was going. "New Year's Eve or Christmas?"

"Oh, you know nobody is going to co-sign on Christmas. New Year's Eve it is," Terrell answered laughing. "This year or next year?"

"Next year. Most of this year is gone. We won't have enough time to plan it out for this New Year's Eve." Jocelyn smiled back at Terrell as she answered.

Jocelyn couldn't concentrate at all at work. She had a wedding to begin planning. She told the people at her job about her engagement and was met with a lukewarm response. She decided to do exactly what Terrell said and forget them. When they asked about the wedding, she told them it was going to be a small family affair. She refused to let anyone's negativity damper her mood.

The phone snapped Jocelyn out of her thoughts.

"So now you are getting married for real?" It was Monique on the other end.

"Yeah, I am going down the line calling everyone and telling people. Who told you? We have only told our parents so far." Jocelyn was very curious about who told her.

"Lawanna told me. She said Terrell came over and told her, throwing it in her face. She is going to cause problems for you," Monique answered flatly.

"Monique, nobody can ruin this for us. We have already talked about it and decided all the negativity stays on the outside. I have a question to ask you though," Jocelyn responded.

"What?" Monique asked.

"Will you be my maid of honor?" Jocelyn asked.

"No," Monique answered quickly. Too quickly.

"Why?" Jocelyn responded. She couldn't believe she was saying no. Is this the same person that got an attitude because she thought she wasn't going to be in the wedding?

"It's too much of a responsibility for me right now. I have a lot going on as well and it is going to take most of my time and resources to handle it," Monique answered.

"What is going on?" Jocelyn asked.

"I'm not ready to talk about it right now, but soon. I will happily come to your wedding, but I can't be in it." Monique offered nothing else and told Jocelyn she had to go. She told her she just called to tell her about Lawanna and congratulate her and Terrell. She hung up before Jocelyn could get anything else out.

Jocelyn thought about her conversation with Monique and wondered if she should say something to Terrell about Lawanna causing problems. The more Jocelyn thought about it the more she realized there was nothing Lawanna could do to get to them. Terrell would handle anything that arose with his son.

She came down a couple of notches from the happiness she was feeling when she got to work that morning, but she was still a lot happier than she had been in a long time. She wondered about what the deal was with Monique. Monique said she would tell her in due time, so she could wait for her to tell. She would not worry about that now. One good thing came out of all the events of the morning: she was able to begin doing her work. She was back on track in that regard.

Just as quickly as she got into her work zone, she faded back out of it. She had a lot of planning to do and knew exactly who to call. Her mother. Her mother was so happy to hear from her. She had some ideas of her own that she wanted to run by Jocelyn. She was about to start when Jocelyn told her that she had the theme and date all picked out and that she and Terrell had discussed it and agreed to it.

Her mother asked exactly what she had in mind and Jocelyn told her. She agreed it sounded beautiful but asked about the practicality of it. Her mother told her she would never get a church to marry them on New Year's Eve. She was shocked and appalled when Jocelyn said they didn't plan to get married in a church but in a hall or a hotel.

"What do you mean you aren't getting married in a church?" her mother asked.

"Well neither Terrell nor I really belong to a church or attend that often so I think it would be awkward to get married in one," Jocelyn responded.

"You could get married at my church. Probably not on New Year's Eve because they have services but I'm sure the reverend would fit you in because you are my daughter. He may want to meet with you and Terrell and give you some pre-marital counseling, but it really wouldn't be a problem." Her mother was digging in and Jocelyn wondered if it was a mistake to call her.

She decided to put her foot down. "Mama, we have decided that we are getting married in a hall or hotel. A church wouldn't be able to transform to fit my ideas anyway."

"OK. I was just trying to make it easier for you. I still don't think New Year's Eve is a practical day to get married." She took her defeat well.

"I will take that into consideration and talk it over with Terrell." Jocelyn wanted her mother to understand this was their decision, not just hers. That way, her mother would be less inclined to knock it down. "So other than the date and the fact it is not going to be in a church, do you have anything else you want to add or provide?"

"No dear. It sounds beautiful and if you want it, you got it. I will do anything I can to help you," her mother answered. Jocelyn thought this was too easy but didn't push it. She told her mother she had to get back to work and hung up.

She thought about calling Terrell and asking him if he thought she was being impractical as well. She also wanted to tell him about Monique and the things she said. She still couldn't believe Monique. Once again, the thought brought her back down to earth, and she dove into her work, deciding she would talk to Terrell when they got home.

Chapter 23

Jocelyn hated to admit her mother was right, but she was having no luck finding a venue or person to marry them on New Year's Eve. She was so disappointed. Why wasn't anything going the way she planned? She didn't want to think of it as a sign. Naw. She and Terrell were meant to be, and everything was going to work out.

She picked up the phone and called Terrell. That's what she needed, to hear his voice.

"Hey honey," Terrell answered. "How are you?"

"Hey. I'm ok. Things aren't going the way I planned but I'm good," she answered.

"What's not going right? Anything I can help with?" Terrell asked.

Jocelyn was taken back by Terrell's response but managed to recover. "I'm having no luck getting anything on December 31st. Apparently that's a busy day. I don't know what to do."

"We can elope," Terrell answered with a laugh.

"Then we'd have to join the witness protection program to avoid being killed by my parents." Jocelyn laughed with him, but she didn't think any of this was funny.

"Can we change the date?" Terrell asked. "A winter wonderland themed wedding on the first day of winter, December 21st?"

Terrell was on a roll, Jocelyn thought. She loved his idea and co-signed to it right away. "Perfect, baby. Thanks. I love it and I love you."

Terrell was happy that she liked the idea. He noticed how much this was stressing Jocelyn out. "I'm glad I could help. Baby, do you need extra help planning the wedding? Like a professional planner?"

"I don't know yet. I'll let you know if it gets to be too much." Jocelyn thought about it. "I need to get some work done. I'll talk to you tonight."

She hung up and asked herself who she was just on the phone with. It sounded like Terrell, but it couldn't possibly be him. He was so supportive and helpful. They'd come so far from his 'anytime, anywhere' attitude at the beginning. She was so grateful for his input.

She called her mother. Terrell suggested hiring a professional, but she wanted to run it by her mother first and see to what extent she could help or if she even wanted to. She knew she would never hear the end of it if she didn't ask her first.

"Mama, you were right about New Year's Eve, but Terrell had a great idea. We are getting married on December 21st instead of December 31st," Jocelyn alerted her mother.

"That's great. Still not in a church, though?" Her mother couldn't resist.

Jocelyn tried to let her annoyance pass before she answered. "No. No church. The reason I am calling you, Mama, is I want to know if you can help me with the planning. Terrell suggested a professional planner, but I would rather do it with you." Jocelyn knew she was pouring it on, but she didn't care.

"Of course, I'll help you as much as I can," she responded. She had a couple of ideas she wanted to slip in. She'd lost out on the church, but she still wanted the ceremony to be more on the religious side. "Just point me in the right direction."

Jocelyn was so happy. She really didn't want to hire a stranger. "Thank you, Mama," Jocelyn told her mother before telling her she had to get back to work. She thought about calling Terrell back to tell him her mother was on board, so she didn't need the professional but decided she had wasted enough of her day on wedding stuff and not enough on work stuff.

At home, Jocelyn and Terrell were both beaming. They both had news for each other. Little did they know that they had the same news. Terrell's mother thought hiring a professional was a silly idea and volunteered to do whatever she could do to help Jocelyn. Terrell warned his mother not to approach the planning with a negative attitude about Jocelyn and she agreed.

Jocelyn let Terrell go first. It was the least she could do since he was being so helpful, and she wanted to let him know that his input was welcomed and appreciated. Terrell told her about his mother and Jocelyn tensed up. She knew she wasn't his mother's favorite person and didn't know how that would work out, but she accepted her help and told Terrell about her mother being on board.

"You know our parents have never met?" Terrell asked. "Imagine that?"

"I never even thought about that but no they haven't. We have to change that," Jocelyn responded. "We could invite all of them here for dinner."

"That's a great idea. I have to call and ask my father, although I know the chances of getting him in the same room with my mother before the wedding is slim to none." Terrell rolled his eyes at the thought. "Promise me we will never be like that. Even if we aren't together forever, we will still remain civil. I don't ever plan a time when we aren't together, but I just don't ever want to end up like them."

"I promise. I guess it's an easy promise to make while we are in love, but I believe we can remain friends in the case of the unthinkable," Jocelyn answered and hugged Terrell.

They stayed hugged up for a while, just holding each other. Terrell began kissing Jocelyn's forehead, but she didn't move. He didn't either. He spoke first, telling her that everything was going to be fine and that their parents helping with the wedding was a good thing and a lot cheaper than a professional. He told Jocelyn he had actually contacted a couple of wedding planners. Jocelyn looked up at Terrell. She was totally surprised and very pleased. Terrell went from 'just tell me when and where to show up and what to wear' to participating in the planning.

Jocelyn showed her appreciation by kissing Terrell's neck and then releasing her hold so she could unbutton his shirt. She told him that this is another thing they needed to promise, no matter what they would not let romance and intimacy fall off in their marriage. Terrell nodded in agreement and began following Jocelyn's lead by taking her shirt off as well. He then picked her up and carried her upstairs, telling her he was getting his carrying down pat for their honeymoon night.

Chapter 24

Jocelyn picked up the phone oblivious to the storm that was coming. It was Monique. Jocelyn kind of hoped she was calling to tell her that she changed her mind about being her maid of honor, but at this point she had no idea what to expect when she talked to Monique.

"Just answer me this one question?" Monique started. "Did you sleep with Mike?"

Damn that was to the point, Jocelyn thought. "No, I did not. Where would you get an idea like that?" Jocelyn asked. She was thrown aback by the question. She knew Monique knew better than that. She would never sleep with Mike. Jocelyn thought about it and decided to add that. "I would never sleep with Mike. You know that."

"I don't know what to expect from you anymore and people said they saw you and him all huddled and hugged up in a bar. Then you left together arm in arm," Monique continued.

"Did any of them see how drunk I was? Mike was only trying to help. He dropped me off at Terrell's house," Jocelyn answered. "Why didn't you just ask Mike?"

"I did. He told me it was none of my business and laughed me off," she answered.

Jocelyn was surprised by that response, but she didn't read too much into it. "So that made you think we slept together? WOW!" Jocelyn responded. "Once again, I would never sleep with Mike. Just in case you need to hear it again!"

"Why did you say it like that? Like you are just dismissing me and the subject?" Monique shot back with an attitude.

"I'm not dismissing you, but I am going to get off the phone. I don't understand what is going on with you but accusing me of sleeping with Mike is a little out in left field. Goodbye, Monique." Monique's nerve surprised Jocelyn.

"So that is it? Goodbye?" Monique asked. Something in the way she said that made Jocelyn know she wasn't just talking about the phone call.

"Monique, what are you talking about?" Jocelyn questioned.

"You haven't been a friend to me in a long time so I think we should say goodbye and call it a past," Monique answered.

"Wow!" Jocelyn said. "If that is what you think and want there is nothing I can do to change your mind or stop you."

"Yeah. You're right. You're always right. Goodbye Jocelyn," Monique said as she clicked the phone off.

Jocelyn shook her head. She couldn't believe what had just happened. She thought about calling Terrell, but he'd told her that was coming for a long time. She decided to call him anyway and see if he'd heard the same thing.

"Hey honey" Terrell answered. Jocelyn remembered that it used to take him forever to answer the phone—if he answered it at all.

"I just had the weirdest conversation with Monique," Jocelyn started. She was almost hesitant about continuing. "She accused me of sleeping with Mike. Remember that night when I got drunk? She said someone told her that we were all hugged up in the bar."

"What?" Terrell asked.

"Yeah. I told her that I was drunk and upset about you and things between us, and Mike was only trying to help. I told her that he dropped me off at your house. Then she came at me on some other stuff and decided she didn't want to be my friend anymore." Jocelyn gasped.

"Are you ok?" Terrell asked. He thought about saying he told her Monique was acting funny but had a second thought not to.

"Yeah, I guess I have to be. What am I going to do?" Jocelyn answered. She really wasn't ok. She couldn't believe what had happened.

"You can give her space. Live your life, she'll come around. If she doesn't then you think of the times you had as friends and know that you didn't do anything to spur this on," Terrell answered.

Jocelyn was once again surprised. Terrell had been showing her some stuff lately. She couldn't hold back the tears anymore. She cried and laughed at the same time. "Thank you."

"For what?" Terrell asked.

"For being here and for not asking me if I slept with Mike," Jocelyn answered.

"I saw you that night. If anything happened, you didn't know about it. I know Mike wouldn't have taken advantage of you. If he would have, he wouldn't have done it and brought you to my house," Terrell said. "I don't know where Monique got her information, but I know it's wrong."

Terrell laughed but knew it wasn't funny. How dare Monique try to start trouble during what should be the happiest time in Jocelyn's life. He had the mind to go tell Monique about herself. She had the nerve to say Jocelyn wasn't a friend. If he didn't know any better, he would think Lawanna was behind this, but he didn't feel like dealing with her so he would let it ride. It was a short-lived rumor and they were good so they would just move on and show everyone that this didn't get to them.

"So, are you sure you are alright?" Terrell asked Jocelyn.

"Yes, I'm good. I'll miss her but you are right," Jocelyn answered. "I love you."

"I love you too," Terrell answered. He wondered where that came from but liked hearing it.

Jocelyn then told him she had to get back to work and she would see him later at home. He could tell that she was still not herself. He could hear it in her voice. He shook his head and decided he would talk to Monique about it. Let her know that she would not ruin their wedding or relationship and that if her girl Lawanna had anything to do with it, that she should call her off.

Terrell called Monique and met her for lunch. When he saw Monique, he knew something was different about her right away. He kept it to himself because he couldn't figure it out. He thought about it and realized she was heavier than he remembered her being. He shrugged to himself and thought he wouldn't be asking about that one. Definitely not something you ask a woman—if she gained weight. Instead, he focused on what he did want to ask.

"What is going on with you and Jocelyn?" Terrell asked, not trying to sound accusatory.

"Nothing now. We've dissolved our association," Monique answered coldly.

"Why?" Terrell asked. "Why now?"

"We haven't been on the same page for a long time," Monique answered. "Jocelyn needs friends and apparently a husband that can play the background to her. It is not a fit for me. It's not a fit for you either, but you'll figure that out." She was smiling now. Actually, it was more like a smirk.

"Maybe I will because right now I don't get it. I don't think Jocelyn is trying to put anyone in the background, especially me or you for that matter. She even asked you to be her maid of honor," Terrell answered. This conversation was confusing him and going nowhere.

"Well, I couldn't possibly be her maid of honor." Monique looked up at Terrell with that same smirk. "I also couldn't tell her why."

"Why couldn't you tell her? Tell me," Terrell questioned.

"I wouldn't have felt comfortable being her maid of honor knowing that her husband tried to be with me in the past." Monique was laughing out loud, laughing in his face.

"What the hell are you talking about?" Terrell forgot all about that. He had to take a minute to figure out if that was true. "That was so long ago, and nothing became of it. That is not the reason."

"I would have had to tell her. I couldn't stand up for her with that information. For a minute I thought she knew and slept with Mike to get back at me." Monique was making no sense to Terrell now.

"You know damn well Jocelyn didn't sleep with Mike." Terrell felt like screaming but held his composure.

"Maybe I should tell her anyway. Let her know what she is marrying. How do you think she will respond to knowing that you tried to break the most sacred bond between best friends?" Monique was still laughing. "Your marriage won't last anyway so we might as well get everything out in the open."

"You know what. Your friendship with Jocelyn should be over because you are not her friend. Good luck to you and whatever is going on with you but stay away from Jocelyn. I'm warning you." Terrell gave Monique one last look before he walked off. Monique was standing there laughing and shaking her head.

He thought about it and wondered if Monique would stoop as low as to actually tell Jocelyn about his one moment of insanity. He wondered if he should tell Jocelyn before Monique could get around to it. Damn. He had forgotten all about it. He hadn't wanted to talk to Monique anyway. He had just wanted to get Jocelyn's attention or make her mad. He figured Monique would have told Jocelyn back then when it mattered.

Just then, picturing Monique's face laughing at him he figured it out. She's pregnant. Her face had the look of someone who was pregnant. He picked up his phone and called Lawanna.

"Who's your girl pregnant by?" Terrell asked as soon as Lawanna picked up the phone.

"Hello to you too, baby daddy," Lawanna answered. "Which girl are you talking about?"

"Damn how many girls do you have who are pregnant?" Terrell laughed the question out.

"If you are asking about Jocelyn, I would say Mike." Lawanna had her own jokes.

"Ha ha, not funny. My fiancée is not pregnant," Terrell shot back knowing that would hurt Lawanna.

"Then who are you talking about?" Lawanna simply asked to his surprise.

"Monique," Terrell answered.

"Not my girl, but I would still guess Mike," Lawanna answered. She was so serious that Terrell thought there was something wrong.

"Oh. I thought you two were close. What's wrong Lawanna?" He asked.

"Nothing is wrong. Why are you asking me that?" Lawanna seemed surprised at his concern.

"You just sound different. Even your joke about Jocelyn seemed half-hearted," Terrell told her. "How is TJ?"

"Everything is fine Terrell. I have just been doing some thinking. I'm sorry about giving you and Jocelyn a hard time. You have been a good father to TJ and good to me," Lawanna said. "Seriously."

Terrell almost dropped the phone.

"I accept your apology. Know that nothing is going to change. I'm still going to be good to you two," Terrell answered, trying to match Lawanna's seriousness. He wondered where this was coming from but thanked God for it. He didn't want to fight with Lawanna and he damn sure didn't want to have to take their son from her. "I don't want to fight with you, nor did I ever want to fight with you. You are a good mother to my son."

"Thank you, Terrell," Lawanna answered. His response surprised her too.

"Lawanna, take care. I am headed back to work. I just wanted to call you and ask if you knew about Monique. I'll be by to see TJ later in the week. If you need anything, call me."

"OK. Bye Terrell," Lawanna responded.

Terrell was pleased and blown away by that conversation. But it seemed like taking one step forward and two steps back. He had the situation with Lawanna squared away but now he had to deal with Monique's crazy, vengeful ass. Where the hell did she get off? Terrell decided he would block it out of his mind and figure out how to tell Jocelyn himself—tonight.

Terrell pounced around the house waiting for Jocelyn to come home. He cooked dinner, cleaned up, and now he was just pacing. He didn't know how Jocelyn would respond to his admission, but he knew he wasn't going to lose her over this. He rehearsed and re-thought what he would say. Damn, he thought, did I do too much? She's going to know something is up. He looked around. It was too late to get rid of what he'd cooked. He told himself to calm down. He was hopping up and down and didn't hear Jocelyn come into the house.

"What's wrong baby?" Jocelyn asked Terrell.

He gave her a shocked look. "Nothing."

"OK," Jocelyn answered. She didn't believe him.

"I need to tell you something." Terrell couldn't even hold it in. "It's something that happened in the past."

Jocelyn just looked at Terrell. She didn't know if she wanted to hear what he had to say. She had all types of things going through her mind. Another child, a wife...all the worst that could happen came rushing to the front of her mind. She went to the couch and sat down. She looked up at Terrell to alert him that she was listening.

"I went to see Monique today. I wanted to get her to lay off you. The meeting didn't go well, and she brought up something that happened in the past and threatened to tell you." Terrell breathed a sigh before he continued. "It was before I even met Lawanna. I was mad at you and felt that would be the way to get back at you. I tried to talk to Monique. I wasn't serious. I didn't even really want to talk to her in that way but thought it was a way to get your attention. I'm sorry."

Jocelyn was kind of relieved, but she didn't tell Terrell that. She wanted to know how far things went so she didn't respond.

Terrell was scared out of his mind. "I didn't even remember it. She said that is the main reason she couldn't stand up as your maid of honor. I am so sorry. I know there are lines that shouldn't be crossed and trying to talk to your best friend was one of those lines."

Jocelyn still didn't respond. She wasn't mad about it and was surprised. She did, however, wonder how Monique could keep this from her all this time. She knew that it was not really the reason Monique was acting the way she was, but she still didn't let Terrell in on that fact.

"Are you going to say something? Silence is worse than anything else." Terrell looked stressed.

"I'm not mad. Did anything happen? Is that why she ended our friendship on the pretense of me sleeping with Mike?" Jocelyn asked.

"Nothing happened. She shot me down cold, and I thought that was the end of it. Like I said, I wasn't even really interested in her and had forgotten about it." Terrell still wasn't breathing. At least he didn't appear to be.

"OK," Jocelyn answered. "What do I smell? It smells so good."

"Oh. I baked chicken. I hope it tastes as good as it smells." Terrell was still checking for signs from Jocelyn. He was nervous, even more than before he told her. She seemed fine but was she really? He didn't know how to ask her. He thought of going to her and hugging her, trying to kiss her or something. He instead went and pulled her chair out from the table and seated her for dinner. He then took the place setting over to the stove and fixed her a plate.

When he brought her plate to her, he reached across her and gave her a kiss. "You know I love you, right? And I wouldn't do anything to hurt you?"

"I believe you," Jocelyn answered. She was still playing coy. Now she wondered how long she could milk this. She looked down at her plate and started eating. It was actually good.

"When did you learn how to cook?" Jocelyn asked Terrell.

"I've always known how to cook," he answered with a smile.

"I thought your mother did all of the cooking for you," Jocelyn inquired. "This is good."

"For the most part, but I could cook." Terrell's breathing was coming back. He felt better but still didn't think he knew how Jocelyn really felt.

"So why did you go to see Monique today?" Jocelyn asked.

"I wanted to ask her what was going on with you two. People don't just throw friends away like that. Did you know she is pregnant?"

"No, I didn't know she's pregnant. Do you think it is Mike's?"

Jocelyn agreed with Terrell. People don't just throw friends away like that. She wondered if that was why.

"I have no idea. I called Lawanna to try and find out and she didn't know either. I guess they aren't really cool anymore." Terrell said before even thinking about it.

"Really? I didn't know them to be that close anyway. Monique told me Lawanna was going to try to cause problems between us. Imagine that," Jocelyn responded. She looked at Terrell and saw the pain in his eyes.

"Oh yeah. Lawanna won't be causing any problems. She actually apologized to me about causing trouble for us and said she won't do it anymore. She shocked me." Terrell was starting to get back to normal. Jocelyn hadn't gotten up and left. No screaming or anything. She said she was fine and he was starting to believe it.

"That's good. A nice thought," Jocelyn answered.

She smiled at Terrell, trying to tell him he was off the hook. He smiled back at her hoping he wasn't misreading her smile. He asked if she wanted more food. She shook her head no and got up to leave the table. Terrell wanted to follow her but instead he put his head in hands and prayed everything would be ok.

Jocelyn wasn't done with the situation though. She wanted to know why Monique never said anything about the so-called moment and picked now to come out with it. If she thought Jocelyn believed for one moment that was the reason she didn't want to be in the wedding, she was sadly mistaken. Before she knew what she was doing, she was on the phone calling Monique.

"Hello?" Monique answered in a voice that seemed weird to Jocelyn. Jocelyn also thought it was weird that she was even answering because she called their friendship over earlier that day. Jocelyn had forgotten all about that.

"So, tell me what happened between you and Terrell. I've heard his side of the story, but I don't believe him." Jocelyn told Monique. She believed Terrell, but she wanted to hear Monique's story. She wanted to see how far-gone Monique actually was.

"It was nothing. I'm sorry I didn't tell you sooner," Monique answered. Jocelyn shook her head. She didn't understand Monique's response. Why did she put Terrell through that?

"So, nothing happened?" Jocelyn asked again.

"No. He just asked if we could go out some time. I said no and he didn't even take it any further," Monique answered. She almost sounded disappointed.

"OK. That's what he said. I just wanted to check the story. How are you doing?" Jocelyn responded.

"Why are you even calling me? Did you not understand me earlier?" Monique asked.

"Yeah, I understood you, but after Terrell told me the reason you didn't want to be in the wedding and that you felt sorry about it, I thought the problem was solved. I don't have any hard feelings about it," Jocelyn answered. She really didn't, but Monique's attitude had her curious.

"No, the problem is not solved," Monique retorted.

"So how can we resolve the problem? You are my oldest friend, and I am not going to let you go that easily," Jocelyn answered.

"I just need time," Monique answered. She was surprised that Jocelyn was actually telling her it wasn't over.

"No. Talk to me. What is going on? Did I do something to you?" Jocelyn asked. She was determined not to let Monique off the hook.

Monique broke down and told her it was hard to watch her get married while she was going through what she is going through. She told Jocelyn about her pregnancy and the father's denial of her child. He told her that he was not making any moves until he saw a paternity test. Jocelyn listened and couldn't help but feel blessed.

She was still smiling when Monique broke into her 'men ain't shit' speech. Then she asked Jocelyn if she really thought she should marry Terrell if he could hide something like trying to talk to her best friend. Jocelyn told Monique that Terrell said he hadn't even remembered trying to talk to her until she brought it up. Jocelyn thought about it after she said it and realized she probably shouldn't have said it to her at that moment. Monique just said "OK" and changed the subject.

Jocelyn didn't know how to take the "OK" that Monique gave her, but she wasn't concerned with that.

"So, are we OK?" Jocelyn asked Monique.

"Yeah. I'm sorry girl. I know I have been tripping," Monique told her.

"I'll attribute it to hormones and your situation, but don't try to bail on me again, especially when my godchild is coming." Jocelyn accepted her apology.

Monique laughed. She hadn't even thought about all of that. At least someone was happy she was having a baby. Monique and Jocelyn talked for a while longer before Jocelyn told Monique to take care of herself and her godchild, telling her she had to square things away with Terrell. She told Monique he was still probably down there, thinking she was mad at him. She promised to keep in touch with Monique before hanging up.

Jocelyn then went downstairs to get Terrell. She went up to him and sat on his lap. This brought a big smile to his face. He wrapped his arms around her and buried his head in her chest. She played with his head and began telling him about her conversation with Monique. He laughed at the whole thing but wouldn't let Jocelyn go. He wanted to hold her to make sure she was there with him. She picked his head up and kissed him on his forehead then on his nose and then lips. She wiggled out of his grip and led him upstairs.

Chapter 25

Jocelyn was running around making preparations. She didn't know why she was so nervous, but she was. She had met Terrell's parents before and Terrell practically lived at her house when they were going out but for some reason their parents had never met each other. She attempted to look for times when it would have been possible for them to meet but decided to stop when she went through a couple and found nothing. She started thinking about later that night and tried to calm down, asking herself what was the worst that could happen. Even if their parents didn't get along it wasn't that serious. They wouldn't even have to see each other after the wedding.

Then she decided she was going to change her thoughts. Everything was going to go fine, and everyone was going to get along. She put on some music and started walking to the kitchen when she heard the phone ring. She looked at the phone, hoping it would stop ringing. She didn't want any bad news or distractions. It didn't stop ringing and when the answering machine came on, she heard Terrell's voice, so she picked it up.

"What took you so long to answer the phone?" Terrell asked in an annoyed tone.

Jocelyn couldn't believe her ears. "What?" she asked.

"Sorry. I'm just dealing with my parents. My father is not coming. That is why I am calling you."

"Well, OK. I'll take the place setting off the table. Did he say why he can't make it?" Jocelyn tried to hide her disappointment.

"Yeah, my mother is a bitch. I think that was his excuse," Terrell answered, frustrated. "He said to give you his best and tell you he'll see you at the wedding but that being in close quarters with my mother is not going to happen."

"Oh. Sorry baby. This night will go by quickly and smoothly and then we'll be alone, and I'll give you a massage and get rid of your stress," Jocelyn answered.

"Yeah, that thought is enough to get me through the day and the night," Terrell said with a grin. "See you in a couple of hours. You know I have to pick my mother up, right?"

"Yes. I'll be waiting." Jocelyn answered.

Jocelyn's parents arrived before Terrell got home with his mother. She explained the day's events and told them that Terrell's father sends his regards and looks forward to meeting them at the wedding. Her parents shook their heads like they understood but Jocelyn knew they had some opinion about the situation. She was just glad they kept it to themselves and hoped they would continue to keep it to themselves when Terrell and his mother arrived.

Terrell came in about an hour later with his mother. She looked around then complimented Jocelyn on her small, quaint house. Terrell rolled his eyes and Jocelyn could tell he was on his last nerve. She thanked Terrell's mother with a smile, hoping his mother would catch a positive vibe and not start with her.

Jocelyn offered to take her coat. She looked at Jocelyn, rolled her eyes and gave her coat to Terrell to hang up. Jocelyn continued to smile, turned, and walked into the living room where her parents were sitting. Terrell came in with his mother and apologized for being late and then introduced his mother to Jocelyn's parents. Terrell's mother looked up at Jocelyn's father and then at her mother before she went to the other side of the room and sat down. Terrell shook his head and walked out of the room.

Jocelyn's mother spoke first, trying to ease the tension. "Well, the kids finally got it together?"

"I don't know. I believe my son can do better," Terrell's mother answered.

Mrs. McCrary rolled her eyes. She was not going to answer Terrell's mother, but she couldn't help herself. "Well, we know our daughter can do better."

As she was saying it, Jocelyn walked into the room and cut her off. "Mama!"

"No, let me finish. I know my daughter can do better but she chose Terrell, and we've accepted that. Terrell has always been like a son to us, so being our son is not a stretch." Jocelyn's mother's look could have burned a hole through Terrell's mother.

Just as she was finishing Terrell came downstairs in a different shirt. He was pleased to hear Jocelyn's mother's words but wondered what his mother had said to provoke it. He decided he didn't want to know. His mother was not going to ruin this night. He put his arms around Jocelyn. She hadn't even heard him come down because of the shock of what her mother had said. She was so happy to hear her mother say it as well.

"I just want what is best for my son and I don't think Jocelyn is it." Terrell's mother wouldn't let it go.

"Mom, you better get on board quickly or get out. I don't care how you get home. Take a cab, bus, whatever but you will not sit in Jocelyn's house, in front of her parents, and disrespect her. Understood? She is what is best for me and lucky for me, I decide that not you." Terrell shocked himself with his response. Terrell shocked everyone. The room was so quiet you could hear a pin drop on the carpet. "Now would anyone like anything?" Terrell asked, looking at Jocelyn's parents with a smile.

They all declined so Jocelyn and Terrell went to the kitchen to put the finishing touches on dinner. He hoped he hadn't been too hard on his mother, but he knew he had to stop it or she would have only gotten worse and ruined the evening for everyone. Jocelyn stole quick glances at Terrell while they were in the kitchen. She wanted to see how his declaration was affecting him. She had never heard him talk to his mother like that and hated that she was the cause of it.

She poured a glass of wine and took it out to Terrell's mother. Terrell's mother gave her a short look and then Jocelyn did something even more shocking. She gave her a hug. "I'm sorry. I know I am not what you want for your son. We've had this discussion before. I'm working on it, and I plan to be there for him for the rest of our lives."

Terrell's mother shook her head and began to cry. She felt bad for the way she acted. She embraced Jocelyn back and apologized for it. Jocelyn wiped her eyes and told her not to cry, and that everything was going to be fine. She told her once again that she understood that she was trying to protect her son.

Jocelyn got up and went back into the kitchen and embraced Terrell. He thanked her.

"She only wants to protect you," Jocelyn told him.

"She is going about it all wrong. Disrespecting you and your parents is not the answer." he said.

"I don't think she meant to disrespect us." Jocelyn really wanted everything to be ok between Terrell and his mother. "Go out there and let her know everything is ok. Don't stay mad at her."

Terrell did as he was told. He went over and hugged his mother. She embraced him tightly. "You know it is hard for me to let you go. You have been it in my life for a long time."

Terrell never even thought about that. He had been his mother's main companion for the past few years. The person who gave her a reason to cook; someone for her to talk to. He looked at his mother in a different light at that moment and felt bad about how he responded to her earlier.

"I'm sure, Mama. I'm sure that Joce and I are going to be ok," Terrell told his mother, his eyes softening. "You can let go."

Terrell went back into the kitchen. Jocelyn looked at him. He just hugged her. He let go and spoke. "Enough of the mushy stuff; we need to get dinner done."

Jocelyn laughed, kissed him and that was all the mushy. They completed dinner, set the table, and then called their parents into the dining room to eat dinner.

Dinner was peaceful. Too quiet was a better description. This was not at all what Jocelyn had in mind. Especially because both mothers agreed to work together on the wedding. Jocelyn tried to think of something to get the conversation started, but she wanted to tread lightly so she didn't start another argument. She thought there was no better subject to discuss than the wedding and what their roles could be.

"Mama, Terrell's mother agreed to help with the wedding planning also. Isn't that great? I'm glad you both have decided to help because I'd rather have my family than a stranger and so-called professional."

"Really? I look forward to working with you," Jocelyn's mother said. She looked directly at Terrell's mother and smiled.

Terrell's mother looked at Terrell and then at Jocelyn's mom and answered. "Yes, we must get together at another time with Jocelyn and go over what needs to be done." She smiled also. This made Terrell smile. He didn't know whether his mother was being sincere, but he is glad she was being diplomatic.

Jocelyn was happy also. "Definitely. We'll make a girl's day out of it, maybe go to the spa or lunch or something."

Both women nodded at Jocelyn's suggestion. Jocelyn's father cleared his throat. "You are just going to leave us men out of it? What do we do, just show up?" he asked. Everyone laughed.

Finally, Jocelyn's mother said, "Yes, honey, you just have to show up. Have your tux on properly and walk well enough to get Jocelyn down the aisle. Terrell will probably do more."

"Gee thanks." Jocelyn's father laughed.

They all went back to eating. Once again it was quiet; too quiet but Jocelyn just let it go this time. She wasn't going to force conversation on them. They had plenty of time to get to know each other during the wedding planning. There wasn't really much to plan because Jocelyn knew what she wanted so they would have a lot of downtime, mostly running errands to make what she wanted to happen, happen.

After dinner, Terrell's mother declined dessert and coffee and stated that she needed to get home because she had to be to work early. Terrell agreed to take her home. She shook Jocelyn's parents' hands and then walked over to Jocelyn and gave her a hug. This was a moving sight. Jocelyn hugged her back and told her she would contact her about the planning and thanked her for coming.

Terrell kissed everyone and thanked them for coming before he helped his mother into her coat and walked with her out of the house. "Thank you, Mom," Terrell said on the way to the car. "Thank you for trying to meet them halfway. I didn't mean to snap at you earlier."

"It's ok. I was out of line but know that I just want what is best for you. I always have," She answered. He nodded and hugged her tightly before opening the car door. "Her parents seem very nice. I can tell they raised her right. I still believe she is spoiled and sheltered but if you can manage that then you should be ok."

Terrell rolled his eyes at his mother but decided not to take her on. Not tonight. The evening had ended on a positive note. That was how he wanted it to stay—positive. He just told her he could handle it and Jocelyn was not spoiled. He also made sure to tell her that the conversation ended there. They rode the rest of the way in silence.

Chapter 26

Jocelyn was pleased with how everything was going. Her mom and Terrell's mom were getting along like two old friends. Terrell's mother even went to church with Jocelyn's parents one Sunday without Terrell and Jocelyn. They thought this was odd until they were cornered by the two women. Terrell's mother went on and on to Terrell and Jocelyn about how beautiful the church was and how eloquent the pastor spoke and how effective his message was. Terrell was pleased with his mother's new faith until she turned to Jocelyn and asked why she didn't want to have the wedding in the church.

The two women had taken it upon themselves to talk to the minister about having the wedding in the church even though they knew that Jocelyn and Terrell didn't want to have it there. Jocelyn's mom chimed in, telling them that it could be held in the recreational room and that it would give the same feel as having it in a hall. The recreational room could also be set up to the specifications that Jocelyn wanted.

Terrell and Jocelyn just looked at each other. Then they looked at both their mothers who were smiling like the Cheshire cat. Terrell excused them and went into the kitchen with Jocelyn to discuss the idea. When they reappeared, they agreed to the solution that the mothers presented. Both mothers clapped and produced the lists that Jocelyn provided them, checking off finding a venue.

The moms huddled up and began whispering between themselves. Terrell and Jocelyn looked at each other again, feeling the other shoe was about to drop. What were those two plotting about? Jocelyn was especially worried because she was unwilling to compromise on anything else on the list, she gave them.

When they broke out of the huddle Jocelyn's mom spoke first. "Since you are having it in the church now and Pastor Green is going to do the ceremony, why not make the ceremony more traditional?"

Jocelyn explained to her mother, "I told you before why that is not going to happen. Terrell and I were brought up differently as far as religion and any religious decisions are going to be made by both of us, not by one of us. If Terrell wants to join our church or any church, he is welcome to do so. But I will not force it on him."

Terrell's mom looked at Terrell and started in. "Terrell it is really a good church with a very good vibe. I was surprised at how much I enjoyed it. You should go check it out. I know you will like it too. I know I didn't give you much of a religious foundation growing up, but I think Jocelyn's mom is right. A marriage should start off with a religious foundation. It gives the couple a better chance."

Jocelyn shot her mom a disappointing look but didn't even look at Terrell's mom. She couldn't believe how her mother had manipulated the situation and that Terrell's mother couldn't see she had been manipulated. Jocelyn was so mad she just spoke, "Take what you got because that is it. Terrell doesn't have to go to church until he is ready and like I said it doesn't matter if he chooses another religion, church, or denomination, I will support him in his decision. He agreed to do the church's marital counseling and work with pastor Green in regard to our wedding and marriage and that is commitment enough for me."

Both the mothers gave Jocelyn a startled look and then looked at each other. "OK, baby," Jocelyn's mother replied. "We just thought it would help. Marriages these days need all the help they can get. We'll get started on Monday trying to make your vision come to life. You won't be sorry about having it in the recreational room either. You saved money and it may be bigger than the average hall."

Jocelyn smiled but knew the war was far from over. She had won a battle and surrendered a battle, but the war was going to be a long one. She could tell by the alliance that her mother and Terrell's mother had formed. She just hoped her relationship with Terrell wasn't the ultimate casualty.

Later that night while Jocelyn and Terrell were watching TV Terrell turned to Jocelyn. "Why did you protest so much about the wedding being religious? It wouldn't bother me if it were."

"I just don't want my mother to overrule everything that I want. I told her before that we wanted it simple," Jocelyn answered. "I'm sorry for the way she is manipulating your mother also."

"Please, my mother is not that easily manipulated. She is getting something out of the deal. Actually, I think going to church has been good for my mother. She seems more positive."

"That's good, but I'm sure that is not because it was in my mother's plan. My mother's plan was to get her there and talk up the church and the pastor so your mother would be on her side when she re-presented the idea of a religious wedding and having it in the church. I will pick and choose my battles with those two, but I want the wedding I planned to have."

"OK. I guess I understand, but if you do want to have a religious wedding don't think because I wasn't brought up in the church that I would oppose it. I would endure any ceremony that ends with 'I now pronounce you man and wife,'" Terrell said with a big grin on his face. Jocelyn smiled back at him, nodding, and taking him in. She couldn't believe that in a few months they would be man and wife. She never thought this day would come.

Terrell saw Jocelyn staring at him and wondered why. "What's wrong?"

"At this moment, absolutely nothing is wrong. I have never been so happy in my life. Thank you, Terrell." Jocelyn answered and kissed Terrell.

"What are you thanking me for?" Terrell asked.

"For being there for me, even when you thought you shouldn't be or that I wasn't down or there for you," Jocelyn answered. She kissed him again.

"You know I always got you. You don't even have to ever ask; just know I got you," Terrell answered before putting Jocelyn's head in his hands and turning her toward him. He kissed her on her forehead and then returned her earlier kisses.

The next day, Jocelyn's mother called and asked Jocelyn to come to the church with her and Terrell's mother.

"I like the fact that you two are getting along. I didn't know how it was going to work out after the night we had at my house," Jocelyn said before agreeing to go with them to the church.

Jocelyn's mother told her she was glad everything was good between them also and that she liked Terrell's mother. "We have a lot in common, despite having different views and upbringings. I am starting to think of her as a friend more than a future in-law."

Jocelyn smiled to herself and began to wonder what the two women had in store for her. She flashed back to the night before and wondered if she was walking into an ambush. She prepared herself for the worst, a meeting with the pastor or something to make her commit to what they wanted: a religious wedding. She wouldn't go into it with a negative mindset, but she would be aware of the possibility.

At the church the women took Jocelyn right past the main building to the back where the recreation center was located. They opened the door which Jocelyn thought was weird because the building was usually locked when no one was using it. Here it comes, she thought, the pastor is going to be in here waiting...but he wasn't.

The two women turned the lights on and began to demonstrate things from Jocelyn's list and showing her how they would look. They had a couple of questions and concerns but said they mainly wanted to see how it felt to Jocelyn. Jocelyn could actually see her vision of her perfect winter wonderland wedding and smiled at the thought of this place being transformed into a winter wonderland.

Some of the questions the women had included the height of the roof and the fact that the room has bleachers for sporting events. They admitted they hadn't thought of that when they presented it to Jocelyn. They were looking more at the cost and the fact that it was located at the church. Jocelyn was shocked at this admission although she knew it was the truth. She twirled around and it came to her.

"How about if we make the bleachers look like the mountains?" Jocelyn was feeling it. "And the fact that the ceiling is so high isn't a problem either because there will have to be lighting to give the impression of winter."

The women looked at each other and discussed whether or not that was something that could be done. They decided it was, so they both pulled out their notebook and crossed something off and wrote something else down. Jocelyn was pleased. She couldn't wait to tell Terrell what was going on. Could it be that this wedding was going to go off without a hitch? Maybe she was wrong to think it was going to be a war.

Jocelyn informed the women she had to make an appearance at the office, and she would talk to them later. She got in her car and looked back before she drove off. She needed reassurance that she was actually where she thought she was. No pastor jumped out at her trying to convince her to have more of a traditional church wedding, and the mothers were suddenly on board with her idea and contributing the way she planned. She shook her head in disbelief but decided to accept it for what it was and be thankful.

Chapter 27

Three months had passed, and while the planning had stayed on schedule, things were not as planned. Jocelyn noticed some of her ideas were being left out. Jocelyn and Terrell's mothers are fighting over how the church recreation room should be set up, who should sit where and how everything should be. They are arguing although they knew these were all decisions Jocelyn and Terrell had already made. Jocelyn attempted to tell them she knew what she was doing and would really like to have the opportunity to participate in the planning of her own wedding.

"Nonsense, Jocelyn. We know how busy you and Terrell are. We don't mind helping," was Terrell's mother's answer. Terrell's mother had actually told Jocelyn she could call her mom. That really touched Jocelyn. She credited her own mother for the change in Terrell's mom and Terrell did also. She was still going to church with Jocelyn's parents and had even begun reconciling with Terrell's father.

Jocelyn's mom's answer was not as subtle. "I'm helping to pay for this wedding, and you are my only daughter so I know you don't think I wouldn't have any input." They also reminded Jocelyn it was her and Terrell who asked for their help.

Jocelyn shook her head in disbelief and walked off. Not so long ago they couldn't even stand each other. Now they are teaming up against her. She really couldn't take it anymore. She just wanted a simple wedding. Short and sweet is what she had in mind but that had flown out the window weeks ago. She was really frustrated but they were right, she and Terrell were the ones who asked for their help.

Jocelyn called Terrell but he didn't answer his phone. This had been going on for a couple of days. Jocelyn thought this was a fine time for him to disappear. It made her question if the marriage was right. She wondered why he wasn't there with her, helping her deal with everything. Her mind wandered back to the other times in their relationship when Terrell disappeared and wondered if it would change after they were married.

They'd talked about it before, and he'd said he would work on it. He was just used to handling things alone. Jocelyn wondered what he had to handle now and why he was shutting her out. She smiled to herself, thinking she was possibly overreacting. The stress was getting to her. She had to pinch herself to believe they'd actually made it to this point. She assured herself that everything was going to be OK and decided to let the mothers fight it out. As long as she was marrying Terrell, everything else was secondary.

Jocelyn called Terrell's phone again and this time she left a message. She told him she was ready to elope. Their mothers were driving her crazy. She giggled into the phone and asked for his help before hanging up.

Jocelyn's next call was to Monique. She explained to Monique what was going on and Monique jumped right in.

"I would call off the wedding. Who do they think they are? Where is Terrell?"

"They are truly tripping and as I said I don't know where Terrell is. I didn't have any plans with Terrell. I just left a message on his phone," I told her, hoping she would understand I just wanted to blow off steam.

"When was the last time you spoke to Terrell?" She asked.

So much for understanding, I thought.

"What? Why does that matter, Monique? What are you trying to imply?" I questioned and let her know I wasn't looking for him until now.

Monique fired back, "OK, because you know how he is. I wasn't implying anything but apparently something is on your mind."

"There is nothing on my mind. I told you those women are just stressing me out. You know what, bye." Jocelyn then turned her phone off.

Jocelyn was on her way to her dress fitting. This was the one thing she had decided to do on her own. She didn't need any help or opinions on that. She knew exactly what she wanted. She had dreamed of this dress since she was a teenager. At first, she thought she would let the women in on the process and ask their opinions but knew there was no room for questions. This was her dress. She thought about it and knew the one person she could talk to about her dress was Monique.

She thought back to the hours Monique and she had spent planning their weddings, down to who they were going to marry. Jocelyn had to laugh because it had always been Terrell for her. She let Terrell choose his own tux and what his groomsmen would wear but she already had that picked out in her mind as well. He did well though. He picked a traditional black tux for all three of them and a tux with a tail for his son to wear.

She thought about Monique and how she hadn't spoken to her in a while. She didn't want Monique to get lost again. She wondered if Monique was getting big; she should be about 5 months. She picked up the phone and dialed Monique's number.

"Hello," Monique answered. She sounded like she had an attitude, but Jocelyn thought nothing of it.

"Hey girl. I was thinking about us and how we used to sit in my room planning our weddings. Do you remember that?" Jocelyn asked. She started laughing but Monique didn't.

"I remember. I guess like in every aspect of our lives you got what you wanted," Monique said with an attitude. Jocelyn still tried to ignore her attitude. She was not going to let Monique get her down, but she did want to know how she was doing and support her during her pregnancy. "Yeah, imagine that. I had given up hope of Terrell and me getting married a long time ago." Then Jocelyn decided to change the subject. "So how is everything with you? Is my God child kicking your butt yet?"

Monique laughed at that. "He is and doesn't like anything I eat."

"Aww. I can't wait to see you." Jocelyn smiled. She was wondering how that was making Monique feel. She remembered Monique wasn't too positive about her pregnancy at first because of the situation with the father. She also wanted to know if that had improved but didn't know how to bring it up, so she just did. "So how are things going with you and Hakim? Is he coming around?"

"Coming around? Do you mean around me or around about the idea that he has a son on the way? Whichever way you mean it the answer is no. He still says it isn't his." Monique sounded ok but Jocelyn knew that had to hurt.

"I'll come see you later this week. We can catch up and you can tell me all about it."

"You don't have to. I know you are busy with your big wedding. I don't want you to feel obligated to visit me." Monique's response cut through Jocelyn.

"Since when do you think you would be an obligation for me? I am coming to see you because I want to. I also want to rub Buddha's belly and connect with my Godson. Obligated?" Jocelyn felt herself getting upset and realized she didn't hide it with her voice.

"I'm sorry Jocelyn. I didn't mean to upset you, girl. I was just saying, I know you are busy." Monique did realize she was upsetting Jocelyn.

Terrell got Jocelyn's message. He didn't call her back though; he called his mom. "What is going on over there? Jocelyn called me asking if it was too late to elope. It is too late to elope, but it is not too late to get a professional who is going to listen to Jocelyn's input about her own wedding. Why would you stress her out?"

Terrell's mother didn't know what to say, so she blamed it on Jocelyn's mother. To her surprise he asked to speak to Jocelyn's mother.

"What is going on? What could the bride possibly want at this time that isn't doable? You know she is talking about eloping? I can't say no to her, so you better say yes to her to keep us from eloping." Terrell figured Jocelyn was joking about eloping, but he wasn't about to tell them that. "It's her wedding and anything short of monkeys flying from the ceiling she gets it."

Jocelyn's mother took the phone away from her ear; who did Terrell think he was talking to? He had put things in perspective, though—she definitely didn't want them to elope. She put the phone back to her ear and heard Terrell yelling hello before she agreed and apologized.

"Don't apologize to me, apologize to your daughter," Terrell stated. He was shaking his head. "I love you. Tell my mom I love her too and will see her when I get home. I didn't mean to disrespect you, but I really want Jocelyn to be happy."

Jocelyn's mother nodded like he could see her. She was smiling also. She was actually proud of Terrell for standing up to her. She was interrupted by Terrell asking if they were good. She told him they are, and she had to call her daughter.

Jocelyn almost didn't answer her mother's phone call but decided she had to. "Yes, Mother?"

"I'm sorry. Come back and show us what you were talking about," her mother told her.

"OK. Why are you willing to listen to me now?" Jocelyn asked.

"A little bird, ok your fiancé, made us understand how important it is to you. He reminded me that it is your day. Were you really going to elope?" her mother asked.

Jocelyn laughed out loud. She couldn't imagine what Terrell told them, but they were shaken. She decided not to answer her mother just in case she needed the "elope" card again. She told her mother she was on her way and hung up.

She called Terrell. "What did you say to our mothers?"

"That's not important. What is important is that they got it and we will be married in front of our friends and family in a few days," Terrell answered with a grin. "I thought your mom was going to cuss me out." They both laughed.

"Where are you?" Jocelyn asked. "Why didn't you call me back?"

"I was in a meeting," Terrell lied, sort of. He was at a realtor's signing the paperwork to close on the house he'd purchased. He prayed she would like it. He tried to get something that would suit her taste more than his. He could live anywhere as long as they were together.

To his surprise she said OK, and let it go.

Jocelyn called and checked in with her mother. She was upset that her plan to have Monique help her with her dress had gone up in smoke. She wanted to ask her mother to come look at the dress but hesitated. Her mother was in a good mood, telling Jocelyn the finish line was near. She asked if Jocelyn was ready. Jocelyn answered, "I'm ready. I'm so happy. I just have to remember that everyone is not as happy as I am, and I am going to stop letting it get to me. I didn't cause their unhappiness and I'm not going to be the scapegoat because things are going well for me."

Jocelyn's mother thought that was a hell of a statement but didn't take her daughter on. She just said, "OK."

"Mom, do you want to see my dress?" Jocelyn asked.

"Yes, of course, I do," her mother told her.

"OK, just remember that this is my dress. I picked it out and there will be no debating it."

Jocelyn's mother was silent for a moment but then told Jocelyn she understood. She did, however, question Jocelyn about why she hadn't let them pay for, or at least help pay for, the dress.

Jocelyn didn't answer her mother's question, she just gave her the time of her fitting and told her she would pick her up.

═══

The dress was more beautiful than she remembered it being. This was definitely her dress; she just hoped her mother wouldn't say anything to discourage it. She didn't know if she could take that. She came out of the dressing room and her mother started tearing up. It was what she'd waited for all of Jocelyn's life; to see her in a wedding gown. It put everything in perspective.

"What do you think, Mom?" Jocelyn asked. She saw the tears in her mother's eyes but wanted to make sure it was a good thing.

"It is perfect. You are perfect. I can't wait for Terrell and your father to see you," her mother answered. She couldn't say anymore, she was speechless. Her little girl was getting married.

"Do you think I should wear a long veil or short one?" Jocelyn asked.

Her mother gathered her thoughts and answered that a long one seemed more elegant, and she should go with it.

Jocelyn was happy with her mother's reaction and input. She knew this was her dress. She couldn't wait for Terrell and her father to see her in it either. She took the dress off, hung it up, and stared at it. She was getting married, and it was just like she'd always imagined it. OK, well, maybe not just like she imagined it, but it still felt good.

With this decision out of the way, it would be smooth sailing. She went to the register to pay for the dress and the woman gave her a strange look.

"What's wrong?" Jocelyn asked the woman.

"It was taken care of by your mother. She paid for it while you were in the dressing room," The woman answered.

Jocelyn looked across the room at her mother who looked as if she'd never moved. "Mom, what did you do? You know I told you Terrell and I didn't need financial help with the wedding."

"But the bride's family is supposed to pay for the wedding. Please let us do this," Her mother's eyes were pleading. "I saw you in the dress and I couldn't help myself. I called your father and he agreed. We were going to give it to you for your honeymoon anyway."

Jocelyn wanted to say no but she couldn't. She loved that her parents wanted to do this for her. She went over and gave her mother a hug. Her mother hoped it meant she was accepting the dress. It did. Jocelyn went back to the cashier and collected her credit card. The woman smiled and set the last fitting up with Jocelyn. It made Jocelyn realize how close her wedding was.

"You still have time to back out," Jocelyn told Terrell when he answered the phone.

"Who is this?" Terrell asked, getting her back.

"Very funny Terrell," Jocelyn answered.

"What? I know it couldn't be anyone I know talking about backing out. In a few days I will be happily meeting my fiancée at the altar," Terrell told Jocelyn. "She better show up."

"Oh, she'll be there. Happily." Jocelyn meant it too.

"Why did you call? Do you need anything?" Terrell asked. "How was dress shopping?"

"I got the dress. My mom paid for it while I was in the dressing room." Jocelyn awaited his response.

Terrell decided he wasn't going to respond. He did, however, wonder why because Jocelyn was so adamant about paying for everything. He did manage to say OK.

"So, what about you? Have you gotten fitted for a tux yet?" Jocelyn asked.

"Yeah. I look good too so you're going have to step up your game. I don't want to show you up." He was amusing himself.

"Trust me you will not show me up. If that was an attempt to find out something about the dress it was a nice try," Jocelyn giggled. "I have to get back to work. I'll talk to you later. Love you."

"I love you too. Can we always remember to say that to each other?" Terrell asked. "I like how that sounds every time I hear it."

"We sure can," Jocelyn answered before they hung up. She shook her head in disbelief. Terrell found new ways to surprise her every day. All the surprises were good now.

Terrell had another surprise when he got home. He announced

that he was moving back into his mother's house until after the wedding. Jocelyn looked at him suspiciously but tried not to see it as a negative. She would miss him, but it was tradition to some people. She nodded yes when he told her.

Tradition wasn't the only reason he wanted to go back to his mother's house. He wanted to help his mother transition to the thought of him not being there anymore. Since they'd been back together, he had been going back and forth, but in a few days it would be permanent. He was worried about his mother being alone.

He also wanted to start furnishing the house he'd purchased. He really hoped she liked it. He showed it to her father, who reminded Terrell of how much she liked her house and asked him what the plan for it was. Terrell told him she could do whatever she wanted to do with it: sell it or keep it and rent it out. That was totally her decision. Jocelyn's father nodded but didn't add any other commentary.

Jocelyn just watched him. She couldn't believe this was the same person she'd met years ago. Then again, Jocelyn saw he wasn't the guy she'd met back then. He was a man now. She was proud of him and proud to be marrying him.

"I'm proud of you baby," Jocelyn said before she realized it was coming out of her mouth.

Terrell looked up at her for a minute. He got up, came to her, and hugged her. "Thank you." He followed that with a kiss. They kissed for a while and decided it was time to go before he changed his mind. They took a long time to break away from each other.

Terrell got to the door and told Jocelyn he'd miss her. She reciprocated and blew him a kiss.

Chapter 28

Jocelyn looked around the place. It was everything she had imagined. The dim, blue lighting gave the full winter, after snow look. She began to cry and left. Her makeup artist would kill her if she ruined the makeup. She had cleverly decided not to put the mascara and liner on, telling Jocelyn she would put that on right before she took that walk.

Terrell just missed Jocelyn. He came in to see the place and what the war had been about. From what he saw it was a worthwhile fight. The place looked amazing. They really captured a winter wonderland. There was make believe snow everywhere and the dim blue lights gave it an almost angelic look. The moms did a great job and he hoped they liked the gifts he left them. He got his mom a puppy, something to nurture, fuss at, and clean up after. It'll be like he isn't even gone, he thought. He got Jocelyn's mother a mother's pendant with room for grandchildren's birthstones.

Jocelyn's father snapped him out of his thoughts.

"You ready son?" He asked.

"Very much so." Terrell answered. "Wasn't always sure we would get here, but happily we have."

"My wife told me you told her off the other day." Mr. McCrary was laughing.

"No, I didn't. I just told her the truth," Terrell answered.

"In a strange way she was proud of you." Mr. McCrary patted Terrell on his back. "Well, you better get dressed."

"See you at the altar." Terrell almost skipped off. He caught himself before Mr. McCrary saw him. At least he thought he did.

He thought about it and didn't care. It was the happiest day of his life.

He wondered what Jocelyn was doing. He'd left her a gift also. He wasn't sure she would get it. It was a diamond pendant with the date around the setting.

Terrell felt his heart drop to his shoes when they cued "My First Love" by Avant and Keke Wyatt. When Avant started singing, he saw Jocelyn come around the corner. He was speechless. She is beautiful, he thought. The dress was amazing, it was a form fitting, mermaid type dress with Swarovski crystals that sparkled in the light on the bodice. She was his first and last love. He thought about the fight they had with their mothers when they found out she wasn't coming out to "Here Comes the Bride." They heard the song and swore it was by someone else. They were right: Angela Wimbush sang it first. He smiled and then looked down because for some reason he felt like he was on his tiptoes. He wasn't. Weird, he thought. He couldn't take his eyes off of Jocelyn.

When she got to the altar, he looked down again. Jocelyn asked why he looked down. He told her he would tell her later and that she looked beautiful before the minister cleared his throat. They both giggled and the minister started the wedding. He was there and listening, but the only words he really heard were "I now pronounce you man and wife." He didn't even remember his vows. He knew he'd said them but didn't remember what he said. He didn't remember Jocelyn's either, so he hoped she wouldn't ask him anything about them until he got a chance to watch the video.

Man and wife, he thought.

"I repeat, you may kiss your bride." The minister said through the laughter of the crowd. Terrell did and they were officially married. Finally!

ABOUT THE AUTHOR

Yvette Way is originally from Boston, MA. A graduate of Curry College with a BA in Communications. She has been writing since a child and has a self-published novel titled "What's A Sista To Do which was released in 2007.

Made in the USA
Columbia, SC
08 June 2025